AN UNCANNY FAMILY RESEMBLANCE

Sarah went over to the cedar chest and pulled out a burgundy taffeta dress with a long, full skirt. "Do you have film in your camera?" she asked her brother Sam. "I want you to take a picture of me."

While Sam went downstairs for the camera, Sarah quickly changed into the dress. She wasn't positive that this was Philippa's dress, but it easily could have belonged to her. It might even have been the very dress she wore to the ball when she met Edwin.

In a few minutes Sam returned with the camera. "I can't believe it!" he said as he began snapping her picture. "You look so much like the painting downstairs. Maybe," he laughed, "you are a reincarnation of Philippa!"

Sarah just sat on the settee, serenely smiling. *She had a wonderful feeling he could be right.*

Other Bantam Skylark books you will enjoy
Ask your bookseller for the books you have missed

ANNE OF GREEN GABLES by L. M. Montgomery

BORN DIFFERENT by Frederick Drimmer

THE CASTLE IN THE ATTIC by Elizabeth Winthrop

DAPHNE'S BOOK by Mary Downing Hahn

FELITA by Nicholasa Mohr

THE GHOST CHILDREN by Eve Bunting

THE GHOST IN THE BIG BRASS BED by Bruce Coville

THE INCREDIBLE JOURNEY by Sheila Burnford

IRISH RED by Jim Kjelgaard

THE MYSTERY OF MISTY ISLAND INN (Haunting with
    Louisa #2) by Emily Cates

THE ORPHAN GAME by Barbara Cohen

SEAL CHILD by Sylvia Peck

TIME AT THE TOP by Edward Ormondroyd

LETTERS FROM PHILIPPA

Anne Graham Estern

A BANTAM SKYLARK BOOK®
NEW YORK · TORONTO · LONDON · SYDNEY · AUCKLAND

RL 4, 008–012

LETTERS FROM PHILIPPA

A Bantam Skylark Book / November 1991

Skylark Books is a registered trademark of Bantam Books,
a division of Bantam Doubleday Dell Publishing Group, Inc.
Registered in U.S. Patent and Trademark Office and elsewhere.

ISBN 0-553-15941-0

Published simultaneously in the United States and Canada

Bantam Books are published by Bantam Books, a division of Bantam Doubleday Dell Publishing
Group, Inc. Its trademark, consisting of the words "Bantam Books" and the portrayal of a rooster, is
Registered in U.S. Patent and Trademark Office and in other countries. Marca Registrada. Bantam
Books, 666 Fifth Avenue, New York, New York 10103.

PRINTED IN THE UNITED STATES OF AMERICA

CWO   0 9 8 7 6 5 4 3 2 1

*To all those young people
whose enthusiastic letters about my books
have encouraged me to continue writing*

❧ CONTENTS ❧

❦1❧

A Family Conference

Underneath the breakfast table in their Connecticut home, the Bingham family pet, a black Labrador named Bingo, rested his head solemnly on his paws. Bingo had been totally ignored these past weeks, and he was very much aware that something serious had gone wrong in the household.

"This isn't going to be easy, but you children are going to have to help me make some very important decisions," Mrs. Bingham said to her children, Sarah and Samuel. It was the first morning since Charles Bingham had died that they weren't surrounded by loving friends and relatives. They each tried hard not to look at the empty chair at the head of the table. But, as if drawn by a magnet, their eyes kept traveling back to it with thoughts of the dearly loved man who had always sat there.

Delicate snowflakes were beginning to float outside the small-paned windows, but no one noticed. They were too absorbed in the sadness that hung heavily in the room.

"Isn't it too soon to start making decisions? We've hardly had time to get used to Dad's being gone," said Samuel.

"I'll never get used to being without my daddy," whispered his twelve-year-old sister Sarah, pushing her half-eaten bowl of oatmeal away.

"I don't think we'll ever get over losing the best husband and father a family ever had. But life must go on for us. Dad would be the first one to tell us that," said Mrs. Bingham gently. She got up to pour herself another cup of coffee so that the children wouldn't notice the sudden wetness in her eyes.

"Do I have to go back to school tomorrow?" asked Sarah. "I'm not ready to do normal things yet. It'll be so hard to keep from crying each time someone tells me how sorry they are that my daddy died."

"Tomorrow is Friday. I suppose you could wait until Monday to start back." Mrs. Bingham sat down at the table and took Sarah's hand. "It's all right to cry, honey. Everyone understands." Bingo put his smooth black head in Sarah's lap and looked up at her sympathetically, trying to show that he, too, understood.

Although only fourteen years old, Samuel felt it

was his responsibility to keep the family spirits up. "So," he said, trying hard to sound lighthearted, "the first important decision has been made! No school until Monday! Anything else?"

Mrs. Bingham stared into her coffee cup, wondering how best to begin.

"What is it, Mom?" asked Samuel. "You can tell us. We're old enough to understand."

"Well," said Mrs. Bingham, clearing her throat, which suddenly felt thick and heavy. "I guess the best thing is to tell you the truth. You see, Dad's illness took almost all our savings. And there's nothing but a small insurance policy coming in. The plain truth is that it won't be long before we're out of money."

"You mean we'll be broke!" said Samuel, stunned at the thought.

Mrs. Bingham nodded miserably.

"Will we have to sell the house?" Sarah asked in a panic. She looked around frantically at the beautifully aged paneling that covered the dining room walls. The sprawling farmhouse had been in the Bingham family since the early 1800s.

"We can't sell the house! That's the last thing Dad would want us to do. He was so proud of this place. He was the one who fixed it up when it was ready to collapse. Why, this house is a monument to him. Besides, it's our heritage!" said Samuel. He too was clearly panicked at the thought of losing the only home he had ever known.

"I hope we won't have to sell the house," said Mrs. Bingham. "I could look for a job but I'm not skilled at anything that would pay well enough to support us. The articles I've been writing for the gardening magazines don't bring in much. Even if I wrote more of them, it would take a long time before I had enough of a reputation to make a real living from them."

"Mom," said Sam, "the house is the most valuable thing we have. If we sold it we'd have to live on the money we got for it. Then when that was used up, we'd have nothing! That doesn't make sense."

His mother nodded unhappily. It was hard for her to see her children burdened with these serious and grown-up problems.

"You know," said Sarah thoughtfully, "Junie Gates's family takes in paying guests. Couldn't we do that? That way, the house could help us earn money!"

"It's true, the house is our chief asset," Mrs. Bingham admitted.

"What a great idea!" said Samuel. "We have three extra bedrooms that hardly ever get used. And we could turn the upstairs sitting room into another bedroom!"

"Lots of people come to visit this part of Connecticut," said Sarah, "and we all know how fast the hotels and inns fill up. Especially in the summer, with all the music festivals and summer theaters."

"And we're right near tennis courts and a lake, and we have the Appalachian Trail practically outside our door," added Samuel. "We couldn't be in a better area for tourists!"

"And," said Sarah, "everyone loves coming to see this old house. Remember how it was the most popular stop on the house and garden tour a few years ago! It's even listed in the book on historic homes of New England. I think we'd get lots of people once the word got around." Sarah looked with new interest at the familiar beamed ceiling and the large fireplace constructed of local stones. There was still an iron hook inside it, left over from the days when all the cooking was done there.

"Are you suggesting," said Mrs. Bingham, "that we run a bed and breakfast business here? Do you realize it would mean sharing the house with strangers? Guests don't rent only a bedroom. They might want to sit around the fireplace in the evenings, or lounge around in the garden. They'll no doubt ask a lot of questions about where to go hiking or fishing or sight-seeing, and we'll have to always be ready to help them. Do you think you're up to that?"

"If running a bed and breakfast means we keep the house, and support ourselves too, then why not?" asked Samuel. "We'd still have our own rooms when we wanted privacy."

"And, Mom," added Sarah, "Dad always said you were the best homemaker and gardener in the state! Ours is the only house I know of that's always ready for guests!"

"Well," mused Mrs. Bingham, "I suppose the one thing I really am skilled at is running a home. And my garden has always been my pride and joy. These are the things, outside of the family, that I've been mostly occupied with for the past sixteen years. I've never been ashamed to admit I enjoyed being a homemaker. But now I may be paying for not having any business or professional skills. Still, running a bed and breakfast business is something I think I can do. And it would leave me time to keep writing my articles."

"We could help," said Sarah. "Sam and I could bake blueberry and cranberry muffins for the breakfasts."

"And I could chop wood for the fireplace, and wait on the tables, and carry in the luggage," said Sam.

Bingo, pricking his ears up at the enthusiasm that suddenly filled the room for the first time in many weeks, trotted happily around the table, stopping at each one for a caress.

Mrs. Bingham's face filled with tenderness as she smiled at her children. "I know I can count on you. But the bed and breakfast better not interfere with your schoolwork."

"That's easy," said Sarah. "We could just get up earlier in the morning and do all the chores before the school bus comes."

"Well," said Samuel, who hated getting up early in the morning, "we'd probably be renting rooms only on weekends or in the summer when we don't have school."

"We'll have to freshen up the extra bedrooms. They're pretty dingy—they haven't had anything done to them in years," said Mrs. Bingham.

"We could paint and paper them, Mom. It won't be the first time we've done it," said Sarah. She remembered how she and Samuel had fixed up their own bedrooms the previous summer. "That's fun work! I wouldn't mind it a bit."

"Me neither," said Samuel.

"Well then," said Mrs. Bingham, smiling with more spirit and energy than she had felt in months, "with all of us pulling together, the bed and breakfast business is sure worth a try!"

"We'll make it work! We have to," cried Sam, waving his mug of hot chocolate in a toast.

Sarah clinked her mug against her brother's in agreement. She looked outside the dining room windows and noticed the now-thickening snowflakes spiraling around in the fields outside. "Look, it's snowing! Isn't it funny," she said, "when you stop feeling sorry for yourself and think about doing something positive, you feel alive and part of the world again. And I feel good knowing Dad would approve."

"Me too," nodded Samuel. "I was feeling as though everything had fallen apart, but we'll get on the track again. Things won't be like they were before, but we're going to be all right. I know it!"

"Yes," said Mrs. Bingham, clearing the table, "I feel better too. And," she added, "we might as well get started. I'll go upstairs and make a list of what we'll need to buy. You two can scrounge around in the attic and bring down a few pieces of furniture we might be able to sell. We've had too much junk stashed up there for generations. We don't need all that stuff, and the antique dealers will pay good money for some of it. We'll need to raise plenty of extra cash if we want to get this place in good shape."

❧2❧

Attic Treasures

"We haven't been up here in ages," said Sarah, pushing open the attic door.

"I used to look forward to rainy days. If we didn't have anything else to do, it was fun rummaging around up here," said Samuel.

"Then we got big, and Daddy got sick, and somehow I forgot all about the attic. I never come up here now except to put away something I don't want to throw out," said Sarah.

"And everything is exactly as we left it." Sam looked around at the cluttered jumble of generations past. "I almost feel nine years old again!"

Sarah nodded in agreement. Entering the attic was like traveling back in time. There sat her old Barbie dolls, starry-eyed and perky, patiently waiting for someone to come and love them again. The Wizard of Oz books had belonged to their father. Both she and Sam had enjoyed them, and now they were stacked in neat and silent piles on the floor. Abandoned to the dust was their old sled, the ice skates that no longer fit, and the blackboard that stood on such spindly legs that it always seemed to be on the verge of collapsing.

Then there were the relics of other Binghams. A delicious-smelling cedar closet held clothes from as far back as the 1800s. Gay silks for parties and somber black taffeta for mourning. A man's striped jacket from the 1920s still bravely sported a dried-out carnation. Even Sarah's baby dresses hung limply in the closet. It was apparent that no Bingham family member had ever been able to get rid of a single piece of finery.

Sarah pulled off the sheet that covered an old horsehair settee sitting in the middle of the attic floor. A flurry of dust scattered around the settee's carved mahogany frame and on the afghan coverlet crocheted in bright squares by Great-grandmother Bingham. Sarah smiled as she remembered the cozy feeling of being wrapped up in that coverlet on cold wintry afternoons as she read about Dorothy from Kansas.

Along the walls and under the peaked roof of the attic stood all the unwanted furniture of the past. A chest of drawers with brass pulls stood next to a marble-topped table and a painted rocking chair. A graceful old spinning wheel and a strange windmill-like contraption cleverly designed to wind wool stood in a corner. Spiders, spinning their delicate webs over and around them, were now the only weavers, working away diligently in the quiet of the attic. Too good to throw away, yet out of style or simply no longer useful downstairs, these relics from another time seemed comfortable and at rest in their attic exile.

"What do you think of this?" asked Sarah, opening the drawers of a pine chest with brass pulls.

"Too heavy to carry down," said Sam, sitting in the rocker to see if it was as comfortable as he remembered.

"Sam!" said Sarah as she peered into the bottom drawer of the pine chest. "There's something inside here I never saw before."

Sam stepped over a trunk to see what Sarah was talking about. "The top three drawers were empty, so we probably never bothered to open the bottom one. Maybe that's why we never saw it before."

"It has EB, 1856, painted on it," said Sarah, lifting out a small painted chest. A lock dangled from an iron strap that held the top firmly closed. She handed the little chest to Sam as she stepped over some hatboxes to get back to the center of the attic.

"Locked!" Sam banged the lid as he unsuccessfully tried to open it.

"Wait, don't break it," said Sarah, opening the

cedar closet and rummaging through the clothes. "I seem to remember a ring of keys on one of the dresses. Maybe we'll be lucky and one will fit!"

"You used to love dressing up in those old clothes," said Sam as he watched Sarah push aside hanger after hanger. "But what makes you think you'll find a key to fit this?"

"Because I think the ring of keys is attached to an apron with an EB embroidered on it. It must be the same EB who owned the chest. I always wondered what the E was for. Of course the B was for Bingham, but was E an Evelyn or Esther or Elizabeth?"

Sam was about to suggest that she give up the search and let him break the lock when Sarah pulled her curly brown head out of the cedar closet with a triumphant smile. "Here it is! I knew it! Now if only one of them fits."

"Give it to me. I'll try it," said Sam.

"No! I get to open it. I found it!" said Sarah stubbornly.

"But I have the chest!" said Sam, about to run off with it.

"And I have this!" said Sarah, dangling the ring of keys. The two youngsters glowered at each other, as neither would give in. "You get to do everything!" complained Sarah as she finally tossed Sam the brass ring. She was more interested in opening the little chest than in continuing the bickering.

Sam fiddled with the lock and the keys. After several tries, a small iron key with a graceful cutout design opened it easily.

"Letters!" cried Sarah, when she saw the pile of yellowing envelopes with delicate writing in brown ink. "A packet of letters! All addressed to a Mrs. Jared Carter!"

"I wonder who she was," said Sam.

"I'll find out," said Sarah, settling herself on the settee and carefully removing one of the letters. The crisp paper was fragile and trying to make sense of the spidery writing was not easy.

" 'Dearest Evangeline,' "

"So that's what the E was for. Who would have guessed!"

"Come on," said Sam. "We don't have all day." Sarah began again. This time she began with the date:

"The 18th of April, 1852

Dearest Evangeline,

England is so beautiful at this time of the year. The trees are in leaf, the hedgerows are bright with foxglove and honeysuckle and the roses are as big as cabbages. I consider myself most fortunate to be visiting our dear relatives in Devon. Their delightful 'cottage' sprawls around a courtyard which has stables and barns built right next to the house. Most remarkable is the roof which is made of woven straw or thatch as they call it here. It appears as though the house has a thick mop of dark hair topping it!

The relatives have been very kind to me. Our cousins, Jane and Geoffrey, seem genuinely pleased to have me here. They take me for rides through the countryside in their handsome carriage. We stop at churches and abbeys along the way so that cousin Jane and I may sketch them. Our home in Connecticut, built in 1803, is very new compared to the buildings here, which date back to the 15th and 16th centuries! I am rapidly filling my portfolio with drawings to bring back home so that you will see some of these unusual sights.

Tomorrow we are going to a fancy ball and supper at one of the stately homes nearby. Dear Aunt Rose has agreed to chaperon Cousin Jane and me. I do hope my burgundy taffeta and my cashmere shawl will be appropriate. I will tell you all about it in my next letter. I have a feeling it will be very different from our church socials, back home.

Embrace your beautiful cherubs for me, and my affectionate salutations go to your Jared and of course to our dear parents. I miss you all.

Your devoted sister,
Philippa''

Sarah sat quietly, transported back to 1852 by what she had just read. "I wonder who Philippa was?"

"Like she said, Sarah, she was Evangeline's sister. But while that letter is all very nice, we're wasting too much time. We have to pick out two pieces for Mom to sell. Remember? Let's get on with it."

"Samuel Bingham, you have no sense of history. That's a letter from 1852 written by one of your very own relatives. Isn't that romantic?"

Sam was concentrating on removing the spinning wheel from the corner of the attic. "Not really," he said in a bored voice. "Here, carry this down." He perched the wool winder on top of a trunk for her and picked up the spinning wheel. "I bet Mom can sell these," he said as he began maneuvering down the stairs with the spinning wheel.

Sarah carefully tucked the letter under her sweater. She laid the key on top of the other letters and closed the little chest without locking it. Putting it back in the bottom drawer of the big pine chest, she patted it gently and whispered, "I'll be back to read the rest of your letters, Philippa."

Grabbing the wool winder, she followed Sam downstairs.

❧3❧

The Story of Philippa

"Oh, Sam, you brought down the old spinning wheel! I'd forgotten all about it. How I hate to have to sell it," said Mrs. Bingham as Sam set it down in front of her. "But," she added thoughtfully, "it wasn't doing anybody any good sitting up in the attic all these years. The wool winder is a lovely piece too. We shouldn't have any trouble selling them. You picked well!"

Sarah gently pulled the letter out from under her sweater. "Mom, we found the sweetest pack of letters in a little chest. You have to hear this."

"Not now, Sarah. I'm starving," said Sam, looking hungrily at the sandwiches his mother had put out on the table. It was the first time in weeks that he actually had an appetite. He poured himself a glass of milk and sat down.

"His stomach always comes first!" complained Sarah as she, too, sat down at the table.

Mrs. Bingham was happy to see the children returning to their normal bantering and complaining. The grief that had been such a heavy presence in their lives was beginning to lighten. Sitting down, she turned to Sarah. "I would love to hear it."

So Sarah read the letter aloud as Sam and her mother munched on their sandwiches. Coming to the end, with the words "Your devoted sister, Philippa," she noticed that her mother had a look of pleasant surprise on her face.

"Why, that must be the Philippa in the portrait!"

"What portrait?" asked Sam, suddenly more interested.

"The one in the living room next to the fireplace. You've seen it every day of your life."

"That portrait!" said Sarah. "You never told us her name was Philippa. I just thought it was some old relative." Running into the living room she looked at the painting more closely than she had ever done before. Created almost a hundred and fifty years ago, the painting had been just another family antique. Sarah had taken it for granted, never thinking of it as a portrait of an actual person who had a name.

"So, you are Philippa," she said to the young woman in the painting. With an intense look of concentration, Philippa in her lace-collared dress, her hair smoothly pulled back from her forehead, stared back. As if seeing the portrait for the first time, Sarah noticed how gracefully the handsome young woman sat with her fingers entwined in a chain from which a gold locket dangled. In the corner of the painting a small doll dressed in a pink and gray calico dress and hat was sitting next to a sewing basket.

Suddenly Sarah put her hands up to her own brown tangle of curls and pulled them back smoothly. Staring intently ahead, she turned to face her brother. "Who am I?" she asked in a mysterious voice.

"Why, Sarah, I never really noticed it before, but you do look a little like the woman in the picture. Especially around the eyes."

"We always thought you resembled the Bingham side of the family," said her mother. "In fact, you are a lot like Philippa in more ways than looks."

"What do you know about Philippa, Mom? You never told us anything about her."

"I'll try and remember some of the family history I used to hear from Great-grandmother Bingham, who loved nothing better than gossiping about the family. Everyone called her Ma Bingham, even though she had grandchildren and great-grandchildren. You children never really knew Ma Bingham because she passed away when you were very little. Dad always said we should have tape-recorded her stories, or at least written them down."

"I wish you had," said Sarah. "Then it wouldn't have taken me all these years to find out that I had a relative named Philippa who wrote letters to her sister Evangeline."

"Philippa was your father's great-great-aunt. That makes Philippa your great-great-great-aunt! As you can see from the portrait, she was quite attractive. No one could understand why she never married. Apparently there were plenty of suitors."

"Suitors! Oh, Mom, what a funny word for boy-friends," laughed Sam.

"In the old days, boyfriends were suitors, and I'm using Ma Bingham's words," said his mother.

"Let's see now," she continued. "Philippa was also very intelligent. She was a fine horsewoman and would ride all over the countryside making a striking figure. She was such a good rider that no one could understand what finally happened to her." Mrs. Bingham paused, as if trying to recall Ma Bingham's exact words.

"What finally happened to her?" Sarah asked in a whisper.

"Apparently she died in a horseback riding acci-dent in England. She was only in her twenties."

"There's something so intense about her face. It's almost as if she knew she was going to die young," said Sarah.

"There isn't too much else I can tell you, except that like you, Sarah, Philippa drew and painted very well. She also sewed beautifully. She made the sampler hanging in my bedroom. If you look closely there is a tiny PB embroidered in the corner."

"I don't believe I'm hearing this! There's a tiny PB scratched in the corner of the glass in one of the windows in my bedroom," said Sarah.

"It was probably put there by Philippa," said Mrs. Bingham. "She was very skilled at all the crafts of the day. Why, she made that sampler when she was about nine years old! Children learned to sew in those days as soon as they could thread a needle. And as you learned from her letter, Philippa was the one family member who traveled quite a bit. She went to visit relatives in England, and in fact she visited the ancestors of the British cousins who stayed with us a few summers ago. Remember Felicity and Jane?"

"How could we forget them?" exclaimed Sarah. "We had such a fun time that summer. And we promised that someday we'd visit them."

"Well, that's out of the question for a while, I'm afraid," said Mrs. Bingham. "Traveling to England isn't cheap!"

"Where did Philippa get the money for her travels?" asked Sam. "She had to go by ship in those days, and it must have been a very expensive trip for the daughter of a Connecticut farmer!"

"Apparently the money came from the tutoring or the sewing she did. Then she got work over there. She became a governess for an English family she met on one of her trips, and she stayed with them for a time.

In fact, I believe she was with that family when she died."

Sarah and Sam sat quietly, looking thoughtfully at the portrait of Philippa. "She was too young to die," said Sarah finally.

Mrs. Bingham nodded. "It's always sad when a young person dies. Oh, yes, there is one other thing I remember about Philippa. It may sound odd, but she had a reputation for losing things! She was famous in family stories for always misplacing something she had worked long and hard at. Like that doll in the picture. Apparently Philippa carved the doll, painted it, and then sewed the clothes for it. No sooner was it done than it was lost. Gone, as if it had dropped off the face of the earth! The family was always very upset about these losses, but Philippa didn't seem to mind." Mrs. Bingham paused, trying to recall more stories about Philippa. Finally she added, "That's really all I know about your great-great-great-aunt Philippa."

They all went back to the dining room to finish their lunch. Mrs. Bingham asked Sam to put the spinning wheel and the wool winder in the car so that she could take them to the antique dealer that afternoon. Turning to Sarah, she asked, "How would you like to help me select some wallpaper for the guest rooms? You have such a good eye."

Sarah nodded. She went upstairs to her room to get a sweater. Looking at the corner of her window, she saw once again the tiny PB etched in the glass.

Although she had seen the initials all her life and had known that some former inhabitant of the room had cut the letters with a precious stone like a diamond or an emerald, she had not paid any attention to it.

"I never knew what these initials stood for, Philippa," she said quietly, rubbing her finger against the letters. "Now I know it was you who slept in this room. You put your mark here. And I look like you! Isn't that all very strange? I can't wait to read the rest of your letters!"

❦4❧

Establishing
The Yankee Spirit

Sam's selection of the spinning wheel and the wool winder was right on target. The antique dealer examined the two old pieces carefully. "You'd be surprised, but I do have calls for these wheels," he said, rubbing his hand appreciatively over the mellow old wood. "Used to be that folks liked them just because they were decorative. Nowadays there are young people who actually spin and produce their own wool. These old wheels work very well and yours is particularly handsome. Some young person is going to be thrilled to own it. I'll be happy to take these off your hands."

While Sarah was pleased to see the nice pile of

bills being counted out, it hurt to see the look of distress on her mother's face as she watched the family heirlooms carted away.

Their next stop was a bit more cheerful. They both felt better after selecting colorful flower-strewn wallpapers that would look perfect in their early-American home. They carefully matched paints to the papers for the woodwork. New brushes, paste, spackle, drop cloths and even some paper painter's hats given to them by the salesman made a bulky package that they stored in the car.

At the fabric shop they bought plain white cotton material and some bright fringe for the curtains. Colorful rugs woven from rags, fresh lamp shades for their old brass candlestick lamps, new sheets, pillowcases, towels, and even new hangers for the closets were purchased.

"Lucky for us," said Sarah as both the car trunk and the backseat were now filled with their purchases, "we already have enough furniture in our guest rooms."

For the next two weeks, they were all so busy they couldn't do anything other than schoolwork and the painting and papering of the guest rooms. They thought often about their father and how he would have guided them through this project with his knowledge and expertise.

"I miss him in so many little ways," admitted Samuel, as he mixed a bucket of paint and worried whether he had added too much water to it. "But it's good to be so busy that you can't stop to think about it."

"I know," said Sarah. "Just when things seem to be back to normal, I run into a problem, and I want to ask Dad to help me. It takes me a few seconds to remember that I won't be asking Dad anything ever again."

As she worked, Sarah thought about Philippa too. She wanted to go up to the attic, snuggle into the settee with the afghan wrapped cozily around her, and read the rest of her great-great-great-aunt's letters. But there simply wasn't time.

Working after school and weekends, Sarah and Sam finally finished putting up the new wallpaper and painting the doors and moldings. The three extra bedrooms and the upstairs sitting room soon looked entirely different. With crisp new curtains made by Mrs. Bingham, the antique four-poster beds covered with handsome patchwork quilts, the freshly waxed old pine chests, and the brightly polished brass candlestick lamps, the guest rooms were very inviting. Sarah, Sam, and Mrs. Bingham were pleased with the results of their handiwork.

"Dad would have been proud," said Sarah, watching Sam wrap up another batch of cranberry muffins in plastic bags for the freezer. She looked wistfully at the brightly polished copper pots hanging from the old kitchen beams. "I wish he could've seen how great we've made the old place look."

Mrs. Bingham nodded as she placed some fine old blue and white dinner plates on the shelves of the dining room cupboard. "He certainly would've been pleased with our hard work and true Yankee spirit. He'd have been very proud of you two," she said as Sam handed her a tray of muffins.

"That's it!" exclaimed Sam. "Mom, you've just named the new bed and breakfast!"

"What are you talking about, Sam."

"True Yankee Spirit! You just said it!"

"True Yankee Spirit? Not bad! But I like The Yankee Spirit even better," said Sarah.

"The Yankee Spirit! Very good! I like it too," said Mrs. Bingham. "It really describes us."

"Okay then! From now on we'll call this place The Yankee Spirit. Sarah, if you draw it out on a piece of wood, I'll paint us a sign. Every inn has to have a sign out front!"

"All we need now are some guests. It's time we started advertising," said Mrs. Bingham. "I'll put ads in all the local papers."

"And I'll bicycle over to the other inns and bed and breakfasts around here and ask them to remember us when they get filled up. You'll see, it won't be long before we're turning them away!"

However, several lonely weeks went by and the warm and cozy guest rooms of The Yankee Spirit remained empty. Sarah and Sam came home from school each day with a questioning look on their faces.

Sadly Mrs. Bingham kept shaking her head. There had not been a single call for a room. Soon it would be spring. She didn't want to worry the children, but she didn't know how long they could hold out without some additional income.

"It's going to take time for us to get a reputation," said Samuel optimistically. "People may have already made their plans for the spring and summer."

"When the leaves turn in the fall, lots of people come to this area," said Sarah. "Why, this town crawls with leaf peepers in the fall!"

"All the prep schools open in the fall too. There are three of them in this part of Connecticut. Won't there be a lot of parents coming up on weekends who are going to need places to stay?" asked Sam hopefully.

"I guess it was too much to expect crowds beating down our doors so soon," said Sarah. "But we can't get discouraged yet."

"What we need is some good publicity," said Mrs. Bingham. "We have to make The Yankee Spirit known. Why don't I write a letter to the local papers and tell them how we all pulled together to create a business to save the house from being sold. Maybe they'll see an angle for a human interest story."

And in another few weeks, a reporter did come over to photograph The Yankee Spirit. She interviewed the Binghams and then wrote a warm story stressing their Yankee ingenuity.

"We've done all we could," said Mrs. Bingham

after reading the article. "It's now just a question of patiently waiting."

"Good," said Sarah. "Now we have some time for ourselves. I'm going up to the attic to read Philippa's letters."

"And I'm going out for a run with Bingo," said Sam.

❧5❧

The Letters

A single shaft of sunlight slanted across the attic as Sarah settled herself on the settee. The little painted chest was in her lap. "This is going to be fun," she thought as she began reading.

It was soon apparent from the letters that Philippa had been a fascinating young woman. She seemed to be skilled at everything she put her hand to. Not only could she draw, paint and ride horseback well, she was also affectionate, intelligent and adventurous. "How I would have loved her," thought Sarah. Evangeline, she gathered, was the more placid and gentler older sister. Married to Jared Carter, Evangeline also lived in the Bingham family homestead with her family. Evangeline was obviously Philippa's closest friend.

Sarah smiled as she read about the ball that Philippa attended wearing her burgundy taffeta dress.

As we stepped down from the carriage, and into the great hall of a most elegant manorhouse, I thought perhaps that I had entered paradise. A thousand candles must have been glowing, musicians were playing waltzes, and the guests were so richly dressed in silks and brocades that I suddenly felt poor and unfashionable. However, with Aunt Rose and Cousin Jane on either side of me, there was no escape.

Seeing my frightened look, one of the guests, a most handsome gentleman, must have taken pity on me, for within minutes of our arrival he was beside me, escorting me into the center of the crowded hall. I no longer felt like the impoverished cousin from provincial America, but more like a beautiful princess graciously accepting the profusion of compliments which were now showered upon me.

My life has changed, dearest sister. This gentleman has quite taken over all my thoughts. We danced away the evening together, stopping only for a bit of supper and a short walk in the formal gardens. I am afraid that he was neglectful of the other guests in order to be by my side. We have many interests in common, and tomorrow we are to go horseback riding through the countryside.

Cousin Jane chastised me for calling my new gentleman friend by his first name, as they are so much more formal in England. However as I had already done so in my informal American way and Edwin seemed quite pleased with everything I uttered, I shall continue to do so.

Edwin lives not too far away in this beautiful Devon countryside. He describes his home as more modest than the one we met in, but I gather it is still by our standards rather impressive. He is known as a country squire here in England. He raises fine horses which are sold to the English gentry. How quaint our own farm and dear little home would appear to him! And yet he was most fascinated with my stories of Connecticut.

Sarah was enchanted! How romantic it all sounded. She conjured up an image of the handsome Edwin, wearing a ruffled silk shirt and a velvet coat, his gold buttons glittering in the light of a thousand candles. He held out his arm to lead the smiling Philippa in a waltz. Sarah, as if she, too, were in the ballroom on that eventful night, felt the music lilting through her head. She envisioned Philippa twirling gracefully around the ornate room, Edwin close at her side. In her mind Sarah walked with them as Edwin led Philippa through the formal gardens. Sarah blushed as she imagined the two of them chatting and flirting under a moonlit sky.

As Sarah read on, she felt closer and closer to Philippa. She, too, was riding through the countryside on one of Edwin's prize horses. She shared the dainty picnic lunches they nibbled together on a grassy riverbank. She walked hand in hand with them through woodland paths and along the shorefront. She laughed at the teasing Philippa endured from cousins Jane and Geoffrey.

Then came the fourth letter. It was a complete shock! A black border was inked around the edges of the letter as if someone had died. Sarah was as upset as Philippa must have been. In a shaky hand, Philippa had written:

Dearest Sister,

Do not mention Edwin's name to me ever again. I have broken off any relationship we might have had. Forget all the nice things I ever wrote about him. He has deceived me. He is married!

My dear sister, believe me when I say that he had in so many ways led me to believe that he was free to form an alliance. And when Cousin Jane, half in jest this evening, said that she supposed there would be a wedding in our family someday soon, he simply hung his head.

Something was very wrong. I knew immediately what the problem was when he said he "wanted nothing better than to marry me, but wasn't free to do so." In a most unhappy fashion I exclaimed, "You are married!" "Yes," he answered, "and no." "Please explain the meaning of that," I demanded.

In a most piteous way, he described a wife who secluded herself in her rooms and sat in a state of melancholia all day long. She never appeared in public and took all her meals by herself. How had he ever married her, I wondered to myself. As if he heard me he responded immediately.

It appears that his father prevailed upon him to form a union with this unfortunate woman, who came from a family of great wealth. In order to maintain his property and home, the father needed the finances from the dowry which would come with her in the marriage. He told me that it was only his filial duty to obey his father that caused him to form this unloving alliance. I surmised that this poor woman wasn't as ill in the first years of the marriage. It was soon afterwards, however, that her melancholia commenced. Perhaps it was when she realized that her husband had no love for her. She has been in this state for five years.

He professes that he never cared about having entered into this unloving marriage until he met me. He knew that it was wrong not to have told me the truth right from the beginning, but he couldn't bear the thought of losing me, or so he states. He also knew that eventually he would be forced to confess, but until Cousin Jane brought up the subject, the scoundrel hadn't the courage to deal with it. Aunt

Rose is beside herself with guilt for not properly investigating the reputation of this dastardly fellow. Cousin Jane swears that she heard no gossip concerning his marital status. It was simply my unhappy misfortune to fall so terribly in love with this wicked man. The saddest part of all is that I truly believe he loves me with all his heart.

But again I beg you, dear Evangeline, never mention his name to me again. I hope I will have the strength to ignore any pleas to see me that he may make. Please destroy this letter.

Your distraught sister,
Philippa

Samuel, bounding up the stairs to the attic after his run with Bingo, found Sarah stunned, rereading the letter. Two large tears rolled down her face. "Oh, Sam," she said. "It's too sad. Read this."

When he had finished the letter, Sam shrugged. "Too bad for Philippa. But all this happened almost a hundred and fifty years ago. Why are you so broken up over it?"

"I feel as bad as if I were Philippa and it were happening to me. I don't know why I'm taking it so hard. I just can't help it," said Sarah.

"Well, I'm glad Evangeline didn't destroy this letter. She saved it so that you could have a good cry over it," said Sam as he rummaged around in a carton of books. Hoping to distract his sister from her saddened mood, he pulled one out, then showed her that it wasn't a book at all, but a box made to look like a book. Inside was an old paint set with blocks of dry paint and a few moth-eaten old paintbrushes. "Get a look at this old paint set. I wonder whose it was?"

"Philippa's. She used to paint and draw," said Sarah without a moment's hesitation.

"How do you know she painted and drew?" Samuel asked.

"She said so, in her first letter. And Mom mentioned it too. Don't you remember?"

"Oh, right, she drew and painted old churches. You sounded so positive that for a minute I thought you really knew Philippa!"

"Maybe in a funny way, I really do know Philippa," said Sarah, putting the letters back in the chest. She went over to the cedar closet and rummaged around until she found what she was looking for. Pulling out a burgundy taffeta dress with a long full skirt, she asked, "Do you have film in your camera?"

"Probably. Why?"

"Would you get it? I want you to take a picture for me."

"Sure. I'll get it," said Sam, pleased that his sister's mood was improving.

While Sam went downstairs for the camera, Sarah quickly changed into the dress. It was almost a perfect fit. Sarah wasn't positive that this was Philippa's dress, but it easily could have been. It might even have been the very dress she wore to the ball when she met Edwin. It certainly was in the style of dresses from the 1850s. Finding some ruffled petticoats in a trunk, she slipped them under the dress so that they pushed the full skirt out in a wide circle. A lace collar pulled out of a box of trimmings completed the outfit. When she discovered two tortoiseshell combs, she propped up an old mirror on one of the chests, pulled her hair back tightly, and stuck the combs in. Her mass of brown curls was now flattened and smooth. Satisfied, she sat down on the settee, arranging her skirt around her gracefully as she waited for Sam.

In a few minutes Sam returned with Bingo trotting behind him. He stared at the sight of Sarah in the taffeta dress waiting patiently on the settee. Bingo stood absolutely still with his head angled to one side in a questioning manner. He was searching for his familiar Sarah.

"I can't believe it!" Sam said as he began snapping her picture. "You look so much like the painting downstairs. Maybe," he laughed, "you're a reincarnation of Philippa!"

Sarah didn't say anything. She just sat, serenely smiling as she posed for more pictures. But Bingo suddenly began acting strangely. Staying close to Samuel, the dog barked wildly at Sarah.

"It's all right, Bingo," said Samuel, patting the barking dog. "It's still Sarah under all those clothes."

Bingo wouldn't stop barking. Finally Sam said,

"You'd better take off that dress, Sarah. You're scaring Bingo, and frankly, you look so much like Philippa that you give me the creeps too. In fact I'm getting out of here," he said, leading the barking dog downstairs.

❧6❧

The Yankee Spirit
Is in Business

Sarah hung the burgundy dress back in the cedar closet. Folding the lace collar neatly, she packed it away with the petticoats. She was about to put the two tortoiseshell combs away when she had a sudden impulse to pop them into her pocket. "I think I like wearing my hair pulled back like Philippa's!"

Sarah returned the little chest of letters to the chest of drawers. "I'll be back to read the rest of these as soon as I can," she whispered.

Down in her bedroom she found Bingo dozing calmly on the oval rug at the foot of her bed where he always took his morning nap. "Now what was all that commotion about, Bingo?" asked Sarah, bending down to scratch his ears. Bingo wagged his tail and licked her hand as he jumped up, eager to welcome her. "What was all that barking about? Did you really think I was someone else? Did you think I was Philippa?"

Sarah sat down on her bed, and the dog nuzzled his head in her lap. Whatever it was that had frightened him was now completely forgotten. "You know, Bingo," she said gently, "I understand how you could think I was Philippa. For a few moments there I really felt like I was Philippa. I just know that was her dress. And I think these were her combs." She turned them over to look at them carefully. She was not at all surprised when she saw, etched in the corner of one of the combs, a tiny PB, exactly like the initials in the windowpane of her room.

"They *are* Philippa's combs. I had a feeling they were hers!" exclaimed Sarah. She was about to tuck them into her hair again when the phone rang.

"I'll get it," she called down to her mother.

The voice on the other end politely explained that they were a party of three couples who wanted rooms in the area for the weekend. They had seen the newspaper ad. Did The Yankee Spirit have anything available?

Sarah could hardly believe what she was hearing. There were people who actually wanted to stay at The Yankee Spirit! They were about to have their first guests! She carefully wrote down the names, confirmed the reservation, and then ran into the kitchen where her mother was washing lettuce.

"We've got guests, we've got guests," Sarah shouted happily, waving the list of names in front of her mother. "Three rooms rented, this weekend!"

Samuel heard the noise and ran inside.

"Yippie," he called out, grabbing Sarah and prancing around the kitchen with her.

Mrs. Bingham smiled with relief. Maybe their luck was changing and The Yankee Spirit would live up to their expectations.

In the midst of the excitement, the phone rang again. This time it was a reporter from one of the larger New York newspapers. She had seen the article in their local paper and was intrigued with the family's ingenuity in establishing The Yankee Spirit. Sarah and Sam saw their mother grinning with pleasure as she was saying, "We'd be happy to be interviewed for your article on bed and breakfasts. Tomorrow would be fine. We'll expect you around four. Thank you for calling."

And so after weeks of impatient waiting, The Yankee Spirit was finally launched. The New York newspaper article raved about the new bed and breakfast. As a result of that glowing publicity, requests for rooms began flowing in. Soon The Yankee Spirit was filled every weekend! Everyone who came loved its old-fashioned charm and comfort. They told their friends about it. Some guests even made reservations to come back again. Everyone was happy!

The Yankee Spirit was so successful that Mrs. Bingham began thinking about the future. How wonderful it would be to enlarge the bed and breakfast business! They had the barn, just sitting there begging to be renovated and turned into at least six more rooms. Then they would never have to worry about money again. They would be able to save for college bills and emergencies, like car expenses or sudden illness. As it was now set up, with only three rooms to rent, the business would take care of all their day-to-day bills and keep them going. It might even be enough for a few luxuries like a vacation now and then. But it would never be enough to provide the extras she wanted for Sarah and Sam. It would take a fortune to renovate the barn, and since Mrs. Bingham could see no possibility of a fortune coming into their lives, she sighed and put away all her plans.

Neither Sarah nor Sam was wild about the cleanup after breakfast, but they both enjoyed waiting on the table. It was also fun meeting the different guests who came to stay. Sam, an eager fisherman, learned all about fly casting from one guest who came several times to fish in waist-high boots in the nearby Housatonic River. Sarah became so friendly with the teenage daughter of a Boston family that a heavy correspondence began. Sam and Sarah baked batches and batches of muffins. There were so many requests for the muffin recipe that they designed a postcard with a photo of The Yankee Spirit on one side and the recipe on the other.

Between school during the week and very busy weekends, Sarah had no time to think about Philippa and her tragic life.

Then, one stormy Friday evening, they were all in the living room waiting to welcome a family coming for the weekend. Samuel was building a fire in the old stone fireplace.

Mrs. Bingham said, "They'll probably be late. There must be terrible traffic in all this rain. You children don't have to stay up. I'll wait for them."

A loud clap of thunder made Sarah shudder. Bingo, as usual in a storm, hid under a table.

"I couldn't go to sleep in all this racket," said Sarah, trying to read.

It was still stormy when they finally heard a loud knocking at the front door. Four rain-bedraggled guests entered. Mr. and Mrs. Chaney introduced themselves and their two red-headed children, John and Martha. Sam figured John to be about fifteen and Martha about thirteen.

"What a welcome sight that fire is," said Mr. Chaney, warming his hands. "And what a wonderful old house this is. It was worth the trip! There were so many cars tying up the roads that we're two hours late. We hope we didn't keep you up."

"That's all right," said Mrs. Bingham. "We're glad you're safe and sound. These roads can be dangerous in this weather." As if to illustrate her remark, a bright flash of lightning filled the living room with an eerie light. Seeing the Chaneys shudder, she asked if they would like a hot drink. "Tea, coffee, hot chocolate?"

"Coffee would be wonderful," said Mr. Chaney. "What about you, Lucille?" he asked his wife, who, he just realized, had been strangely silent since they entered.

Lucille Chaney was staring at the portrait of Philippa.

"Who was this?" she asked in a curious voice.

"Mom, Mrs. Bingham wants to know if you'd like a hot drink," asked Martha, embarrassed at her mother's lack of attention.

"Where did you get this painting?" Mrs. Chaney demanded, ignoring her daughter.

"That's a portrait of one of our father's ancestors. It's been in our family for over a hundred and fifty years," Samuel explained.

"Why does that painting interest you so?" asked Sarah nervously. Somehow it bothered her to see a stranger so curious about Philippa. She didn't want to share Philippa's story with anyone outside the family.

"You're not going to believe this," said Mrs. Chaney, "but when I've unpacked I'm going to show you something that I'm positive will fascinate you. And yes, thank you. I would love some coffee. I'm sorry I seemed so rude. I know these children of ours would like hot chocolate if it's not too much trouble."

Samuel was already showing Martha and John the rest of the house. They were laughing and talking as if they had known each other for years.

Sarah, however, was very quiet. She couldn't imagine what Mrs. Chaney had to show them. Walking into the kitchen to help her mother, she said, "I have a funny feeling that something weird is about to happen, Mom. I'm not sure I like that Mrs. Chaney."

"Sarah, you don't have to like all our guests. But you do have to be polite to them. Remember that!" said Mrs. Bingham.

"Of course I'll be polite. And John and Martha seem very nice. I just don't like anyone staring that way at Philippa." She stacked the coffee cups and saucers noisily on a tray and held it out to her mother.

Mrs. Bingham laughed. "I didn't realize you were so sensitive about Philippa. Mrs. Chaney is only admiring the painting. There's no harm in that. It's not as if she was staring at you." Mrs. Bingham added some napkins and a platter of cookies to the tray Sarah was holding.

"Well, it *feels* like she's staring at me!" Sarah marched into the living room and set the tray down on the pine blanket chest they used as a coffee table.

Mrs. Bingham shook her head as she took the coffee and the hot chocolate off the stove. Sarah was silly. She was too possessive about Philippa. "Why, she was even wearing her hair the same way Philippa did, with the very combs that belonged to her," she said to herself. Aloud, she called, "Come and get it, everybody. And try some of Sarah's cookies. We're very proud of our Sarah's baking talents."

"Oh, Mom, Sam helped too," said Sarah, who blushed as her brother led Martha and John back into the living room in time to hear that last remark.

Martha sat down next to Sarah. "This is such a nice house. We live in an apartment in New York City and it's so different. It's all modern with lots of chrome and a marble entrance hall and a doorman. We have an elevator, but we don't have an attic or a cellar. Do you have an attic?"

"We do," answered Sarah, adding quickly, "but no one's allowed in it. It's a mess." She passed Martha a cup of hot chocolate.

Samuel sat down on the other side of Martha. He was certainly being attentive to the tall red-headed girl he had just met. "Well, we are allowed in it. Sarah means it's sort of off-limits to guests. But if it's raining tomorrow I'll take you up there. We always used to spend rainy days in the attic when we were little."

Sarah turned to give Sam a hard look. No matter how nice he thought Martha was, she didn't want him taking her up to the attic. She was about to say that the attic really wasn't very interesting and that there were so many other things to do that were better, when a loud clap of thunder again shattered the atmosphere.

"The storm seems to be getting worse. I'm glad we're here and not on the road," said John, taking another cookie.

Mrs. Chaney finished her coffee and stood up. "May we see our rooms, please. I'm dying to unpack so I can show you something."

John, Samuel, and Mr. Chaney carried the luggage upstairs as Mrs. Bingham led the way.

Sarah took the tray of cups back into the kitchen. Her attitude softened when she heard the Chaneys exclaiming with pleasure as they discovered their pretty bedrooms. But she didn't know why she had a funny feeling in the pit of her stomach about Mrs. Chaney.

7

An Amazing Coincidence

With the Chaneys upstairs unpacking, the house was quiet again. Samuel banked the fire and let Bingo out for his evening walk. He waited for the dog at the front door and announced that he was getting sleepy.

"Sam, you have to stay up a little longer," said Sarah, hearing the dog whine to come back in out of the rain. "You heard Mrs. Chaney say that she has something very special to show us. She's coming downstairs after she unpacks."

"And in fact she's right behind me," Martha announced as she, too, entered the living room. "Wait till you see what she has! You're in for a surprise!"

47

Sarah was getting more and more anxious. Sam didn't seem to share her fears at all.

Mrs. Chaney walked triumphantly into the living room, waving a small blue-velvet box high over her head like a trophy. Sitting down in a large wing chair, she beckoned the children to gather around. She waited patiently until Mrs. Bingham came in from the kitchen. Mrs. Chaney was fully enjoying the suspense she was creating.

"Martha is absolutely right," she said. "This is an amazing coincidence." Very slowly she opened the velvet box. A gold locket lay inside.

Sarah's eyes widened in astonishment. Samuel caught his breath. Mrs. Bingham's hands clapped against her face. No one expected what they saw inside the velvet box!

It was too incredible! The locket inside the box was exactly like the one in the painting of Philippa!

"But that's not all," said Mrs. Chaney to the stunned Binghams. She was about to remove the locket from the box when another flash of lightning zigzagged dramatically across the sky. The electric lights went out. Martha screamed.

"Don't worry," said Samuel quickly. "The lights always go out in a storm. Sometimes they come on again in a few seconds. If not, I'll get the kerosene lamps. We're well prepared for this kind of emergency."

And as if illustrating his comment, the lights obligingly popped on again. Martha, reassured, relaxed.

"Nothing, not even lightning, is going to keep me from showing you what's inside this locket," said Mrs. Chaney, laughing. She waited as the little group regathered around her before removing the locket from the box. Then, pressing a tiny catch, she caused the locket cover to spring open. There, fresh as the day it was painted, was a miniature portrait of a young woman!

"Oh no," gasped Sarah. "This is too much!" The young woman in the locket was Philippa! There was no question about it! The dark, intense eyes stared at them from the locket just as they did from the painting on the wall.

Obviously, the miniature painting in the locket was a copy made from their portrait of Philippa! But when? Where? How?

"Where did you get that locket?" Samuel finally asked.

"In England. At a flea market," answered Mrs. Chaney calmly. "I think it was somewhere in Devon. It's a real treasure!"

"Would you . . . sell it?" Sarah asked hesitantly.

"Oh no, dear. This locket has been my pride and joy. It happens to be one of those rare finds you come upon once in a lifetime. No, I wouldn't sell it even though I can understand your wanting to buy it. But you have the painting. This is only a copy of the painting. I don't suppose you would want to sell the painting?" she asked cautiously.

"Of course not! We wouldn't ever part with the

painting," said Sarah. "But I wonder how that locket and little painting came to be made."

Mrs. Bingham, recovered from the shock of recognizing Philippa in the locket, reminded Sarah that Philippa went to visit relatives in England. "In Devon, in fact. She may have given the locket to one of the cousins and it eventually was sold. Mrs. Chaney by a strange coincidence had the good fortune to be around to buy it."

"Philippa used to paint," said Sarah thoughtfully. "Maybe she actually did this herself." She took the locket from Mrs. Chaney and examined it closely. John Chaney reached in his pocket, pulled out a small leather-covered magnifying glass, and handed it to Sarah. "This comes in handy at the oddest times!"

Sarah squinted through the glass gratefully. "Whoever painted this must have used a magnifying glass." It took her only a minute to find what she was looking for. There, in the corner, so small that even with the glass she could barely make it out, was a tiny PB, just like the PB's on the tortoiseshell combs and her windowpane. "She did paint it! See, there are Philippa's initials!"

"Miniature painting was very popular back then," said Mr. Chaney. "It was quite a skill, and a number of artists perfected it. And you're quite right, Sarah. The artists used a magnifying glass and a brush with only one or two hairs to paint them. People treasured these tiny paintings. They were generally gifts to loved ones. This one is painted on ivory. Because the locket had a cover, the painting never faded or chipped and is probably in the same beautiful condition it was when it was made a hundred and fifty years ago." It was clear that Mr. Chaney knew all about the miniature and appreciated it as much as his wife did.

"This was not painted by just any artist," said Sarah. "This was done by our great-great-great-aunt, Philippa Bingham. Isn't there some way we can convince you to part with it?"

"Now, my dear, you're making me sorry I showed it to you. Of course I can see how you would want to own it, but do try and understand my position. I happen to love this piece!" Removing the locket from the box, she slipped it around her neck as if she feared that it might fly away.

"It's only a locket, Sarah," said Samuel soothingly. "It should be enough for you to know that it exists. You don't have to own it."

"Strange bits and pieces of Philippa's life are all beginning to suddenly appear," said Sarah. "I can't help feeling that there is some, some . . ." She faltered for the right words. " . . . some reason . . . some message . . . in all of these happenings."

Mrs. Bingham laughed. "I'm afraid our Sarah has a romantic streak. She looks so much like Philippa that she seems to be identifying with her," she explained to the Chaneys. "But I must admit that it's a remarkable coincidence that Mrs. Chaney bought a locket that exactly matches our painting. Of course, coincidences do happen, as we all know! And now," she said, rising to collect the empty cups, "while all this is most interesting, the Chaneys are probably very tired and surely want to get some sleep. Just tell us when you would like breakfast tomorrow morning."

"If it's a nice day, we'll be up around eight o'clock," said Mr. Chaney. "Mrs. Chaney and I are going antiquing. John and Martha want to do some hiking."

"I'll show you some of the Appalachian Trail," offered Samuel quickly. "There are several sections of it around here."

"Great," said John. "It'll be more fun if you two come."

"And if it rains, you can show me your attic," said Martha.

Sarah mumbled something about not being sure what she had to do the next day, but Sam was so noisily enthusiastic that no one paid any attention to her hesitancy. As good nights were said and she went upstairs to her room, her only thoughts were of the miniature painting in the locket. Had Philippa really made it for one of her cousins in appreciation for the hospitality she received? Or had she given it with love and affection to Edwin before she discovered he was married?

The rain had stopped and the night sky was clearing. The clouds, rolling rapidly across the sky, made way for the moon to spread its silvery light on the freshly washed meadow. Opening her window, Sarah looked out dreamily. The apple trees behind the house trembled gently, as if trying to rid their rain-soaked leaves of water.

"All my life I've loved looking out my window in all the different seasons. Yet tonight I feel it's different." With her finger, Sarah traced the tiny PB etched in her windowpane. As she mused, she conjured up what Philippa must have seen when she looked out this same window those many years ago. In a flash, the old apple trees became tiny saplings. The woods beyond the meadow miraculously cleared. She could see right down to the brook where cows were gathered, quenching their thirst in the sparkling water. To the left, a stone wall, neatly stacked, edged the field in an even row of rocky perfection. On the other side of the wall, in an enormous vegetable garden, a scarecrow perched high on a pole. A small barn with lilac bushes next to the door sat comfortably nearby.

Sarah smiled at the vivid picture she had created. "We still have the barn, Philippa, although the lilacs are gone, and woods grew up where your cows were grazing. The stone wall isn't as neatly stacked as it was in your day, but it's still there, solid as ever."

Crawling into bed, Sarah laughed at herself. "Here I am, talking to Philippa as if she could hear me! A year ago or even a few months ago I would've thought I was going batty. But now I don't even think it's strange. Even Mrs. Chaney's locket doesn't seem odd to me. It's as though that locket, because Philippa made it, just had to surface finally, right here in this house. Somehow finding Philippa's letters has set off a peculiar chain of events, and now there's no telling where it will lead. I just know there has to be a reason for all this."

Sarah heard the lights in the other rooms click off one by one. The silence of night slowly filled the house. Lying there in the moonlit room, Sarah couldn't stop thinking about Philippa. Suddenly she popped out of bed, put on her robe and slippers, grabbed her flashlight, and quietly padded out of her room. She tiptoed up the attic stairs.

"I better bring down your letters, Philippa," she whispered. "If that silly Sam really does show Martha Chaney the attic, I don't want her poking into them."

In a few minutes Sarah was back in her room, clutching the small chest. Still not sleepy, she propped up her pillows and made herself comfortable. The letters were on the bed beside her. She began reading.

☙8☙

More Letters

The first letter Sarah picked up was one she had read before, telling of Philippa's first visit to England, and dated April 1852. Sarah smiled as she reread the now-familiar description of Philippa's first impressions. The next was written almost a year after the tragic black-bordered letter. Sarah learned that Philippa had been home during that winter and had just returned to England. Sounding once again like her old cheerful self, Philippa wrote that she now lived not too far from the home of her cousins.

My dearest Evangeline,
     You will be happy to know that I have found employment. I am the governess to a small child called Winnie. Although as timid as a jackrabbit, she is a

most intelligent five-year-old, eager to learn everything I can teach her. For reasons too involved for me to go into, this poor child has been raised thus far without much love and tenderness in her life. Therefore I find it most gratifying to see her blossom under the new circumstances I can provide her with. I have become very attached to Winnie in the short time I have been here.

I look forward to hearing from you. Need I say that I am sorry to hear that your dear husband is not feeling well. I trust he shall have improved by the time of your next letter to me. I eagerly await news of the entire family. Embrace your beautiful cherubs for me.

Your loving sister,
Philippa

Sarah picked up another letter, written several months later that same year. This one was full of pleasant tales of the rewarding experiences Philippa was having with her young charge. It was becoming clear that Philippa loved the little Winnie as much as if she were her own daughter.

The next letter Sarah read was written in October 1853.

Dearest Evangeline,
It was with great distress I read that your dear Jared has not improved. I understand the concerns

you have. I trust that he will have a turn for the better when the weather clears. It must be difficult for you to manage everything with only our elderly parents to assist you. I wish that I could be of greater aid to you, but I cannot leave here. My young charge is too dependent on me, and would suffer greatly if I were to abandon her at this time. We have become very close these past few months, almost as if she was the child I never had.

We go riding each day and the little one has become quite an able horsewoman. I am so proud of her! She has great curiosity and does her schoolwork remarkably well. I have even begun teaching her to embroider. You would be amazed to see her tiny fingers fly in and out of the linen so adeptly. She is making a sampler, much like the ones you and I made as children.

So, my dear sister, please embrace the family for me, and tell your dear Jared that I am praying for his recovery.

Your loving sister,
Philippa

Sarah found herself dozing off, but nothing could stop her now. Shaking her brown curly head to keep herself awake, she continued.

The next one was a short letter written a few weeks later on December 5th, 1853.

My dearest bereaved Sister,

How it grieves me to be so far from you at this moment. Your beloved husband is gone, and you are suffering the anguish of your loss. I do hope the children are of comfort to you at this time. I cannot express my sorrow adequately.

Our parents are too old to take your Jared's place on the farm, but perhaps you can get a hired man to assist you. I am sending whatever money I have saved to be used to aid you.

With a heavy heart I embrace you all.

Your loving sister,

Philippa

Poor Jared! He must have been a fairly young man. Sarah felt great sympathy for the grieving Evangeline. She well knew what it was like to lose someone dear.

Just one more letter! How could she go to sleep now. Delving into the lives of her long-dead relatives was so compelling! She would really have to stop after this last one, for she could hardly hold her head up.

January 12th, 1853

My dearest Evangeline,

My heart breaks for you and your struggles. The severe weather you are experiencing is adding to your troubles. How I wish I was with you. I will definitely return in the spring to help with the chores which will surely be too much for you to accomplish alone. It is a pity that you cannot find a hired man to assist you.

Perhaps I will bring my young charge back with me. I shall broach the subject with her father, who is now home from his business travels.

You say that I have made a mystery of the family I am employed by. Someday I will tell you more about them. For now, suffice it to say that the mother is an invalid confined to her room, and the father is often away. It is clear that he loves the child dearly, and will do everything possible to make her happy.

Now, dear Evangline, I want to tell you something that may be of assistance to you should you need it before I return.

Last winter when I was home I put something away for emergencies such as yours.

Think back to our childhood. You can, I hope, still recall our own secret means of communicating with each other. I will use that old method to impart this important information, as I am fearful of mail going astray. Indeed, I shall be sending it off with a fervent prayer that it doesn't fall into the wrong hands. What you find is of course yours to use as you see fit.

Your loving sister,
Philippa

Sarah turned to the next letter. Where was this

secret message Philippa mentioned? She carefully flipped through the unread letters. The only thing unusual was a separate page that contained a kind of nonsense poem. It reminded her of the "Jabberwocky" poem in Lewis Carroll's *Alice in Wonderland*. Totally baffled, she read:

> Stickety wickety seventeen nickety
> Todel podel about face pickety
> Onkety ponkety hobbledy wonkety
> Nohso whoso yeaso donkety
> Each to his own.

> Wickety stickety seventeen nickety
> Addle paddle about face pickety
> Lohso wohso yeaso donkety
> Lohso wohso yeaso donkety

> Never to seek means never to find
> Evie uncover what I have in mind.

Sarah read it again very carefully. It still made absolutely no sense. "The secret communication!" she said aloud. "That's what it is! It may take time, but I'm going to figure it out!"

Sarah put the poem and the letters back in the little chest and reluctantly put out the light. In the darkness her thoughts rambled through the letters she had just read. Like Evangeline, she, too, thought it was odd that Philippa never mentioned the family of her young charge. Why had she never told her sister the name of the family she was working for? And who was this father who was away on business so much? Big questions for such a late hour. Sarah sighed and fell into a deep sleep.

❧9❧

Sarah's Dreams

Sunshine streaming in through her bedroom window in the early-morning hours woke Sarah with its bright warmth. Drowsy, she lay in bed in a half-awake, half-asleep state. Thoughts of Philippa and the letters she had read the night before crowded her head. She tried desperately to fall back into a deep sleep, but her thoughts continually returned to Philippa.

Suddenly the painting of Philippa began to take shape in her mind. Stroke by stroke, the painting grew under her eyelids as if the artist was creating it for her alone. When the painting was completed, Sarah watched in fascination as Philippa stepped gracefully out of the picture frame and began walking slowly around the room. Tenderly, Philippa touched the various pieces of furniture and even the etched PB in the windowpane, as if recalling things from her past. Satisfied, she came over to sit on the edge of Sarah's bed. In a voice as gentle as a summer breeze, she whispered, "Sarah, uncover what I have in mind!"

Sarah froze! Those were the words in the last line of the nonsense poem. Except that they had been addressed to Evie. "Who was Evie?" she asked. Philippa smiled and took her hand. Her touch was as delicate as a piece of silk woven of cobwebs.

"Evie was the childhood name given to Evangeline."

The vision was so real that Sarah sat up, sweaty and tense. She could actually feel the delicate imprint of Philippa's hand on her own. She expected to see Philippa still sitting on the edge of her bed. But the early-morning sunlight made it clear that she was alone. Philippa was gone.

Restlessly tossing about with thoughts of her strange dream, of the childhood code, and of Philippa and Evangeline, Sarah finally dropped off to sleep again. It seemed to be only seconds later that her mother's voice was calling cheerfully. "Time to get up, Sarah. It's seven-fifteen!"

It turned out to be a beautiful sunny May day, perfect for a hike. After breakfast she watched as her mother packed up sandwiches and a cold Thermos of fruit punch for a picnic lunch for the hikers. Sarah intended to go up to the attic and work on the secret code in the nonsense poem as soon as they all left. But

John and Martha were so excited about going out on the Appalachian Trail that they urged Sarah to join them.

"I can't. I've got work to do."

"What's so important that you can't go for a hike on a beautiful day?" asked her mother.

"The letters," Sarah said pleadingly. "I want to read through Philippa's letters."

"Come now, Sarah," said her mother, annoyed with her for preferring Philippa's letters to a hike. "Surely the letters can wait. John and Martha are only here for the weekend. The letters have been and will be here for a long time. I think it's much better for you to stop concerning yourself so much with Philippa, and go out for a day in the fresh air."

"C'mon, Sarah," said John. "It'll be so much nicer if you come too."

Sarah was torn. She loved hiking, and John and Martha were very nice, and maybe her mother was right. The letters could wait!

"Okay, you guys win. I'll put on my hiking boots and be ready in five minutes!"

"Great," said John, pleased at her decision.

Although her thoughts occasionally slid back to the letters and the code, Sarah enjoyed herself. Sam, walking ahead with Martha, left her to chat with John as they hiked through the well-marked woods. John was a good storyteller and fascinated her with tales of the big city. He wanted to know all about her life in a small town in Connecticut. Sarah felt so comfortable with the lanky city boy that she told him about their father's death a few months before and how they had only recently established The Yankee Spirit. She told him about the letters from Philippa that so fascinated her. She even found herself telling John about the code.

"From the minute I met you I guessed there was something you weren't talking about," said John. "You seemed to be so preoccupied. Even while you were listening to me I felt that you were thinking other thoughts. It's like part of the time you were either someone else or somewhere else!"

Sarah was surprised. Had Philippa so invaded her spirit that it was noticeable to others? She made an even greater effort to keep her thoughts in the present so that she could stop thinking about the past.

It was Sarah's sharp eye that discovered the perfect place beside the stream to stop for lunch. Taking off her hiking boots, she waded in the cool water and invited the others to join her. Perched on a high and dry flat rock in the middle of the stream, they ate their sandwiches as their feet dangled in the crystal-clear water.

It was a great day for all of them. Samuel hated to see the warm and relaxed camaraderie among the four new friends end, but he had to suggest they start back. He had promised Mrs. Chaney that they would return by five o'clock.

As they trudged along, John asked Sarah if she would show him the code. "I used to be good at figuring those things out. It was kind of a hobby of mine. I even used to make up my own codes. I can't promise, but maybe I can help you."

While Sarah hesitated to share Philippa's code with anyone else, she realized that it was more important to solve the secret message. And if John knew something about codes, maybe together they could uncover the secret message quicker than she would by herself.

"It'll be terrific if you can help. I haven't spent too much time on it, but I couldn't make heads or tails of it. I'll show it to you later," she promised.

Sarah had some other questions for John. "You've been to the Devon countryside. That's where your mother said she bought the locket. Tell me about it."

John described the trip they had taken the year before. They had driven through several counties in Devon. They had stayed at bed and breakfast establishments very like The Yankee Spirit. He described the jagged cliffs of Cornwall and the rough waters that washed the shore. He told of the moors at Exmoor, where they had gone horseback riding.

"That's what Philippa did all those years ago," interrupted Sarah.

"And we saw great old houses that were hundreds of years old. Some were castles—they were so grand. The government owns a lot of them now. They became too expensive for the original families to keep up.

That's why they're now open to the public and tourists get to see them."

"Edwin's family resorted to making their son marry for money so that they could keep up their home. That marriage broke my great-great-great-aunt's heart."

"We also did a lot of antiquing because of my parents' interest in old things. That's when we bought the locket."

"Someday I'll go there and see all the places Philippa went to," said Sarah. "I'm going to write to our cousins in England. We used to write all the time when we were littler. And they were here on a visit about four years ago. They're from the same family Philippa visited all those years ago."

The exit from the trail came into view. They were now not far from The Yankee Spirit. Resting on a boulder, they waited for Sam and Martha to catch up. Sarah marveled at how easy it was to be with John. The hours had flown by.

"I had a wonderful day," said John. "I'd like to come back again. I don't mean just the Appalachian Trail. I'd like us to be friends."

"I had a good time too," answered Sarah. "I hope I didn't bore you with too much babble about Philippa. I just don't seem to be able to stop talking about her. Since I learned about her, she's almost always in my thoughts."

"I understand. I would be the same way. I sure hope I can help you break that code."

The others came into view and together they continued on their way. They arrived at The Yankee Spirit just as the Chaneys, their arms full of packages, were getting out of their car. After a whispered consultation between the children and their parents, Mr. Chaney said, "We see how well you all got along. Would you like to join us for dinner this evening? We've made a reservation at that nice country inn in your village."

"We'd love to," Samuel was quick to answer.

"We'll have to check with Mom, but thank you," said Sarah.

"The reservation is for seven o'clock," said Mrs. Chaney as she walked into the house, hugging her purchases. "We should leave at six-thirty. See you then!"

"That leaves us an hour and a half. I can get ready quickly and maybe you can show me that code," John said to Sarah.

"What code?" asked Sam and Martha at the same time.

"Get dressed. Meet me in the living room. I suppose if I'm showing it to John, I might as well show it to you too," said Sarah.

❧10❧

A Lovely Day

"How fancy do we have to dress?" Martha asked Sarah as they climbed the stairs together.

"Casual. Just no jeans."

"Good, I'll be ready in ten minutes."

In her room, Sarah went over to the window and once again traced with her finger the PB etched on the pane. "I love to touch your initials, Philippa. It makes me feel so close to you. I hope you don't mind my showing your letter to other people," she whispered. "I really would never do it if I didn't need help figuring out your code."

As she popped into the shower, she thought about her new friends, the Chaneys. They were nice, and they all got along well. She smiled as she thought of

Sam and the obvious crush he was developing for Martha. But then, John was nice too, she admitted to herself. She hoped they'd come back to The Yankee Spirit soon. It was strange that they had come at this particular time and brought the locket. Maybe fate would play another trick and have them help her break the code.

Slipping into a flower-patterned skirt and a fresh white blouse, she brushed her brown curls into shiny smoothness. She pulled her hair tightly back from her forehead and tucked in Philippa's combs. "Somehow, Philippa, you are always with me in one way or another," she said to her reflection in the mirror. Making faces at herself, she took on the serious look of the portrait downstairs. She gazed at her solemn face and saw once again her strong resemblance to Philippa.

Suddenly she drew back. Was that Philippa or Sarah she was looking at? Was it her imagination or was that actually Philippa's face reflected back at her? Fascinated and horrified at the same time, she stared as the face of Philippa began to actually speak. "Sarah, uncover what I have in mind," the ghostly reflection in the mirror whispered.

She was still staring at the mirror when a knock at the door brought her back to reality. Philippa disappeared and her own image once more was reflected back at her. Relieved, she greeted Martha, who stood in her doorway, scrubbed and smiling.

"The boys are downstairs already and your mother

was happy to let you go out. Now, what's this code you were talking about?"

"You'll see," said Sarah, putting her arm around her new friend's waist and leading her downstairs.

In the living room, she carefully spread out the letter containing the nonsense poem on the blanket chest. They each read it to themselves. Then Sarah began reading it aloud. They all joined in, making it sound like a weird voodoo chant.

> Stickety wickety seventeen nickety
> Todel podel about face pickety
> Onkety ponkety hobbledy wonkety
> Nohso wohso yeaso donkety
> Each to his own.
>
> Wickety stickety seventeen nickety
> Addle paddle about face pickety
> Lohso wohso yeaso donkety
> Lohso wohso yeaso donkety.
>
> Never to seek means never to find
> Evie uncover what I have in mind.

Mrs. Bingham walked in as they were chanting. "What on earth are you doing?" she asked.

"Mom, these words were in one of Philippa's letters and we think it's some kind of code. We were trying to figure it out," explained Sarah.

"Philippa again! Enough already! You're becoming absolutely obsessed with Philippa," said Mrs. Bingham, her forehead crinkling up with annoyance. "You must stop this foolishness!"

"Ready, everybody?" asked Mr. Chaney as he entered the room.

"I wish you could join us, Mrs. Bingham," said Mrs. Chaney as she came downstairs. "Are you sure you won't reconsider?"

"Thank you. It's very nice of you, but I have to stay here. We're expecting some new guests this evening. But the children, especially Sarah, can use a night out. I don't believe they've been to a restaurant since my husband got sick! I really appreciate your taking them!"

Sarah carefully folded the letter and ran upstairs to put it away in her room.

"Direct me, kids," said Mr. Chaney before launching into an involved conversation with Mrs. Chaney about something they had purchased that day.

Squeezed close to Sarah in the backseat of the car, John whispered, "If that poem really is a coded message, it's going to take some doing to figure it out."

"You're going to have to cool it about Philippa in front of Mom," said Sam. "In fact, I agree with her. You really are getting much too involved with all this Philippa stuff. Why, she even dresses up in Philippa's clothes," he said to John and Martha. "I'll show you some pictures I took of her wearing Philippa's dress. You'd swear it was Philippa!"

"Samuel," said Sarah, "if Philippa left a message for Evangeline to help her out, then she probably left money or something valuable for her to find. If Evangeline understood the message and found whatever it was, then we'll have wasted our time. But suppose Evangeline never found whatever it was? She didn't destroy the poem as she was instructed to if she did find it. Maybe all these messages from Philippa are coming to the surface for a reason. Maybe the time has come for us to find Philippa's treasure! Just think what it would mean to Mom if we unearthed a real treasure. Why, she'd be renovating the barn before you could count the money!"

"Maybe Philippa's spirit won't rest until her message is understood," said the romantic Martha.

John was more practical. "If you believe in spirits and ghosts, then all these coincidences have a meaning. Personally, I don't know whether I believe in such things."

"You take a right at the stop sign, Mr. Chaney," Sam called before he turned back to Sarah. "I like the way you assume there's a treasure hidden somewhere. Even if there was one, don't you think that after all these years, someone unearthed it? If not Evangeline, it could have been any one of a dozen relatives who've lived here."

"Oh, Sam, you have absolutely no imagination," said Sarah. "It seems to me that a treasure might just as easily have remained hidden all these years. Anyway, that's the way I prefer to think about it!"

"Whether you do or you don't discover anything valuable," said Martha, trying to keep peace in the car, "it's fun to try and figure out the code."

"It won't be easy," said John, running his fingers through his red hair. "You have to experiment, using the first letter of every word, or the second, or the third, to see if anything makes sense. Then there's a mix of real words and nonsense words in the poem. Maybe the real words are meant to mislead you or maybe they're part of the message."

"I think 'seventeen' must mean seventeen feet or paces," said Sarah. "And then 'about face' obviously means turn back. That's what makes me think there's a treasure stashed away somewhere. I think there's a location hidden in the message. But seventeen paces from where? We just can't go around taking seventeen paces from anywhere."

"That's where the code comes in," said John.

"There's the restaurant, up ahead on the left," called Sam. "You can park in the back."

Thoughts about the code were dropped as they entered the pretty little country inn. A table near the window had been reserved for them. They had a view of a wild waterfall that tossed a mass of foamy white bubbles into the stream below. The Chaneys were as delighted as if the restaurant had been created for them alone!

After they had ordered, Mrs. Chaney dominated

the conversation with questions to Sarah and Sam about the area, their school, and their friends.

When she could, Sarah mentioned the Chaney family's trip to England. Mrs. Chaney cheerfully switched subjects and began to describe the wild countryside in Devon, with its small villages, thatched-roof cottages, and wonderful restaurants!

"The fishing and the hiking and the horseback riding were the greatest," said Martha, turning to Sam. "You'd love it!"

"I'm sure we would. But the chances of our going to England in the near future are practically nonexistent." Sam laughed.

Sarah wasn't so sure about that! There were those English cousins! When they had last seen them several years ago, they had all promised to get together again. She resolved to write to them as soon as possible. She was more determined than ever to arrange a trip to the area Philippa had lived in during the 1850s.

As she studied the dessert menu Sarah put aside thoughts of Philippa and sighed contentedly. Chocolate pecan pie! How fabulous!

It had been a lovely day. They had gone on a great hike, they had new friends, and they were eating a terrific dinner. They hadn't broken the code, but that would happen. Sarah was positive of it. She turned her full attention to the shimmering wedge of pie the waiter had just set in front of her.

❧11❧

An Invitation

Mr. and Mrs. Chaney went for a walk to work off some of their dinner. The four young people gathered around the fireplace back at The Yankee Spirit. Sarah put the nonsense poem back on the blanket chest and Samuel gave them each a pencil and some paper.

They studied, they scribbled, they mumbled, they compared methods, yet no one could make any sense of the nonsense words. It was very frustrating.

Finally Sam threw down his paper. "Maybe that's all it is. Just a bunch of crazy words. Maybe this isn't the message sent to help Evangeline. Maybe Evangeline destroyed the real message."

"I give up, too," said Martha, reluctantly putting down her pencil.

"I've tried every combination and elimination I

can think of," said John mournfully. "I keep coming up with zilch. Maybe Sam and Martha are right, Sarah. This may not be a coded message after all."

Sarah held on to her paper. She folded it up with the letter. "I won't give up. If it takes me a year, I'm going to prove that this is a message from Philippa describing the location of something terrific."

John laughed. "I admire your stubbornness, Sarah. And I hope that when we come up here again, you'll have it solved. I'll fiddle around with it, too, even though I am pretty discouraged."

"Mom and Dad made a reservation for us to come back one weekend in the fall when the leaves are turning," explained Martha. "They've liked it here as much as we have. I wish we could stay longer, but we have to be on our way after breakfast tomorrow. Dad's got some work he has do back in New York."

The four of them swapped addresses and promised to keep in touch.

Upstairs in her room Sarah carefully put the letter back in the little chest. As she undressed she thought again about the Chaneys. Even though the code hadn't been broken, the evening had been pleasant, and she was sorry they were leaving. She looked out her window at the star-filled night sky. The dew was sparkling on the grass like a field of little diamonds. Absentmindedly she traced Philippa's initials with her finger. She imagined herself traveling about the English countryside that John Chaney had described so well.

Suddenly Sarah caught her breath. Her heart seemed to race into fast forward. For the second time that evening, Philippa stared back at her. It was almost as though every time she rubbed the etched initials, Philippa would appear like the genie in Aladdin's lamp. This time the image was tiny at first, then it got larger and larger until Philippa completely filled the window. Her intense look softened as she smiled at the frightened look on Sarah's face. Philippa reached through the glass to take Sarah's hands in hers.

"Go to England," said Philippa in a soft but urgent voice. Then the image slowly faded from view.

Sarah's hands turned icy cold. Rubbing them together to warm them, she wondered whether she had dozed off and dreamt those last few minutes. Or had she actually seen Philippa's ghost? Was Philippa hovering about, ready to pop into the present at any time? Or was this just her own vivid imagination?

She was wide awake now. There was no sense even trying to fall asleep. Going over to her desk, she pulled out some airmail stationery and began a long letter to her English cousins, Felicity and Jane. She hadn't written to them in over a year, so she had much to say to bring them up to date. She told them of their father's death. She wrote about The Yankee Spirit, and how it was becoming a successful business. She suggested that they would love to visit. Late summer, next Christmas, or Easter vacation would be good for them. She sealed the letter and put it on her dresser to mail the next morning.

By now she welcomed falling into a deep and dreamless sleep.

The next morning was a busy one. The Chaneys and the new guests who had arrived the night before were all down to breakfast at once. Conversation at the table was lively. Sarah and Sam's blueberry muffins were, as usual, a big hit. Sarah packed up four extras, which she gave to the Chaneys as they waved good-bye.

The house was suddenly very quiet. After cleaning up the breakfast dishes, they looked around for something to do.

"I better get to my homework," said Sam. "We were having such a good time that I never gave it a thought all weekend."

"Me too," said Sarah as she put away the last glass. "I have to do an essay on a woman I admire greatly."

"Don't tell me, let me guess," said Sam, smiling at his sister.

"Well, why not? Everyone else in the class will be doing people like Harriet Beecher Stowe or Eleanor Roosevelt. But I feel I really know Philippa better than anyone else. And she was courageous for her time! She traveled by herself and took a job in a strange country when women were supposed to stay at home and be domestic." Sarah started upstairs.

"Sarah," Sam called after her, "you don't pay any attention to us but I have to say it again! You really are dwelling on Philippa too much. It's even getting boring!" But Sarah had already closed the door of her room.

They quickly settled back into their routine. Homework, chores, school. Business at The Yankee Spirit was excellent. They were booked every weekend through October! Mrs. Bingham relaxed now that their finances were healthy. Sam started a side business making birdhouses in his spare time. Sarah painted them in bright colors and they sold them easily to guests or to the village gift shop.

Sarah enjoyed writing the essay so much that she illustrated it with several drawings of Philippa in some of the dresses from the attic. She also included the photograph Sam had taken of her wearing Philippa's burgundy taffeta dress. When her mother complained again about her spending so much time with Philippa, Sarah smiled and said that her teacher loved what she was doing. Mrs. Bingham couldn't argue with that!

Each afternoon after school, Sarah went through the day's mail to see if there was a letter from the English cousins. She had received several letters from John Chaney, who, like her, still had no luck in figuring out the code.

Then there it was. A pale blue square of airmail paper appeared in the mailbox the day before school was out for the summer.

Felicity and Jane had been happy to hear from her. They now understood why Sarah had not answered their last two letters. Tears came to Sarah's eyes as she read how saddened they were to hear about Uncle Charles. Sarah realized once again how much she missed her father.

The next part of the letter stood out as if in red ink.

Would Sarah and Sam like to visit them during the last two weeks in August?

She ran to find Sam, who was tossing a Frisbee with Bingo. He was as thrilled with the invitation as she was.

Mrs. Bingham thought a trip to England was a fine idea too. It would be good for Sarah to get away from her obsession with the letters from Philippa. And every penny they earned didn't have to be saved for the barn renovation. The children deserved some fun. It had been a hard year for them.

"You don't have to worry at all about me," she said cheerfully as Sam and Sarah wondered if she could handle everything by herself. "I can ask Annie Small to come in each morning to help me straighten up. And thanks to your efforts, we don't have to worry about the money for the airfare. You've both been so wonderful about everything since Dad passed away. I think he would agree that you should have a special vacation. I'll see about airline tickets this afternoon."

Sam and Sarah accepted their mother's praise with

a sort of embarrassed pleasure. They liked being told that their father would approve of all they had done. Somehow his being gone made it even more important that they act in a manner he would have been proud of.

"And now I have to finish pruning my roses," said Mrs. Bingham, gathering her shears and putting on her gardening hat. As she closed the door behind her, Sam turned to Sarah. "I never thought it would happen. We're actually going to England!"

"Just like Philippa," said Sarah, "I intend to visit the small towns in Devon. I want to try and find the manorhouse where Philippa met Edwin. I want to look for the house where she worked as governess to Winnie. I want to find out more about her death. I'll know her even better if I see all the places she lived. Maybe we can even solve the mystery of the code over there."

"I'd just like to have a good time," said Sam. "It'll be fun to be in another country and see new things. I don't ask for anything more than that."

"Somehow," said Sarah, "I feel I was destined to poke around into Philippa's life. It's not just that I look like her. It's as though Philippa, with her funny habit of walking in and out of my dreams, has given me a special mission to accomplish!"

❧12❧

A Visit to England

With school out, July and the first weeks of August passed lazily by. Sam and Sarah spent their mornings making and painting birdhouses, and baking muffins to store in the freezer or to sell to the country store in the village. They were pleased to be able to earn some extra spending money to take to England.

In the afternoons they swam or played tennis or just hung out with their friends down at the lake. Thoughts of Philippa were always on Sarah's mind. She reread her letters so many times she practically had them memorized. She scrounged around in the attic looking for something that might have been Philippa's for a clue to the nonsense poem. However, she finally gave up on trying to solve the code. She simply couldn't figure it out. And the excitement of the trip to England began to occupy her thoughts more and more as the summer wore on.

The day to leave finally arrived. Sarah and Sam were thrilled and excited as they belted themselves into their seats on the plane bound for England. Neither of them had ever flown before, so everything, from the tiny plastic dinner trays to the earphones for the movie, was fun for them. They took turns at the window seat so that each could admire the world below, spread out like a wonderful patchwork quilt. When they began flying above the clouds and over the ocean, Sarah said, "I feel like I'm in heaven!"

Aunt Emma was at the airport gate with Felicity and Jane. They hugged and kissed and laughed at how they all had changed. It had been four years since the English cousins had been to America!

Jane, at eighteen, was impressively grown-up. She had just learned to drive, so she and Aunt Emma took turns. Sarah and Sam tried to accustom themselves to seeing the driver on the right side of the car instead of the left, the way it was at home. Jane and Felicity laughed each time Sam shuddered at the sight of cars coming toward them. They were headed from the airport directly to the town of Wells, in Devon, where the cousins lived.

"It's so nice the way you edge the fields here with flowering hedges," said Sarah. "In Connecticut we have stone walls along so many of our roads."

"Some of these hedges are actually made of ancient stones," replied Jane. "They were put together with earth instead of mortar. Plants like foxglove and honeysuckle take root in them, making the whole wall look alive."

"In Connecticut," Sam added, "the soil was so rocky the first settlers had to do something with all the stones they dug up when they cleared the fields. That's why we have so many stone walls. Some on our property are over two hundred years old!"

Jane laughed. "In your country two hundred years is considered old. Here we have stones carved and set up by men two thousand years ago. And"—she pointed to some ruins high in the hills—"that's what's left of a castle from the fourteenth century. Now that's old!"

The next few days were spent getting reacquainted, bicycling all around the town, having lunch in thatched-roof inns, visiting the famous cathedral in Wells, and just walking around the quaint, cobbled streets of the town.

Felicity and Sarah were the same age. Felicity loved hearing stories about Philippa. She wanted to know all about the young American woman who had come to visit her own ancestors over a century ago. "She must have stayed here in Wells, because our family has lived here for two hundred years. But our ancestral home was torn down because it was ready to fall down, at least fifty years ago. It was a big house, but nothing like the home Philippa must have lived in when she was a governess. I don't know how we could find out if that house is still standing without names of people or towns to give us a clue. It probably was quite near here or at least within an hour's drive by horseback or carriage."

When Aunt Emma suggested that they take a ride out to the moors of Exmoor and Dartmoor, Sarah was thrilled. Somehow she felt that this was the direction Philippa might have traveled.

"As long as you're patient with me when I stop and look into some of the antique shops along the way," said Aunt Emma, "I'll be happy to take you tomorrow."

"Oh, Sam loves antique shopping," Sarah said, with a twinkle in her eyes. She knew full well how much Sam hated poking around dusty antique shops!

They started out early the next morning. Aunt Emma really meant it when she asked them to be patient with her. They were walking casually around the third antique shop when suddenly Sarah stopped. A small carved doll dressed in handmade clothes had caught her eye. A tag hanging from the doll's arm said, "Hand-carved in America, circa 1850, for a child with the initials E.M."

"It's exactly like the doll in the portrait!" exclaimed Sarah. "Sam! Come look!"

Sam, by now thoroughly bored, wanted only to get back in the car and on their way. Reluctantly he strolled over to where Sarah, almost in a trance, held the little doll.

Sam gasped. His eyes practically popped out like marbles! "I'll be darned! . . . It *is* exactly like the doll in the portrait. But what's it doing here? Wasn't it supposed to be one of the famous things Philippa 'lost'?"

"Maybe she didn't lose it. Maybe she brought it over here. Whatever it was, I must have this doll!" Sarah began counting out the British money she had exchanged for her hard-earned dollars. Two pounds short! She gave Sam an agonizing look. With a huge sigh he reached into his pocket and gave Sarah what she needed to buy the doll.

"Oh, Sam, you're the best brother anyone ever had! I love you!" Sarah exclaimed.

"It's probably only similar to the doll in your painting, and it's terribly overpriced," said Aunt Emma cautiously. "But I suppose you do have to have it since you're so convinced it's the doll in your painting."

"Aunt Emma, this doll is dressed in pink-and-gray-printed material just like ours. Of course it's very faded, but it's the same pattern. I'd recognize it anywhere! And the doll has the same funny little face. I just know this was Philippa's doll!"

"Sarah," said Sam thoughtfully, "if that's really the doll Philippa made it should have her initials somewhere. Didn't she always put her special mark on the things she made?"

Sarah turned the doll over and looked under the dress at the yellowed undergarments. At the hem of the petticoat, embroidered clearly in green thread, was "to EM." But she couldn't find the PB she was looking for.

"Turn to the back of the head," said Jane. "That's where doll makers usually put their initials."

And there it was, carved into the back of the doll's neck at the edge of the hairline! A tiny PB just like the PB Sarah had so often traced with her finger on her windowpane!

∽13∾

Local Gossip

"You've bought a lovely doll, young lady," said the antique dealer as he wrapped it up in tissue paper. "Will you be taking her back to where she was born? You are American, aren't you?"

"I'll be taking her back to the very home she was born in," said Sarah.

"Could you tell us where you got this doll?" asked Samuel.

"Oh, she came in with a large lot of things. People cleaning out an attic, I guess. Can't tell you their names. Paid them cash for the whole mess."

"Then you don't know where they lived, I suppose?"

"No, no. Somewhere around here, I would imagine. People don't travel very far to sell items like this."

They left the shop with Sarah happily hugging the tissue-wrapped package. What a find! Philippa's doll! She couldn't believe her good fortune.

By now the others were hungry. Sarah of course was too excited to think about food! Aunt Emma took them to an inn in an old stone cottage nearby for lunch. After they had ordered, Sarah couldn't resist unwrapping the little doll and holding her up for the others to admire. The waitress came over to see what they were making such a fuss about.

"Oh, she's a dear thing, she is! Where ever did you get her?" she asked.

When Sarah told her, the waitress smiled. "Then I know where she came from. That shop down the road is full of things they've dragged out of the old manorhouse. You know, the one up on the hill overlooking town. New folks bought the place and they've been clearing it out for a year now. You wouldn't believe how much stuff I've been watching them cart out of there."

"Do you know the name of the old family who lived there?" asked Sam. Sarah held her breath expectantly.

"Not a clue. I came to this town only recently myself. But I'll ask the innkeeper for you. He's the local historian around here. And quite a gossip, I might add. Be careful what you tell him!"

In a few minutes, the innkeeper appeared, wiping

big red hands on his white cook's apron. "Who wants to know about the old house on the hill?" he asked.

Sarah showed him her little doll. "I do. I want to know where she came from. I just bought her at the antique shop down the road."

The innkeeper pulled up a chair, turned it backwards, and sat down. Resting his chin on the chair back, he held the doll at arm's length as he squinted one eye at it.

"Looks to me like you got yourself something from the old Moreland place. See," he said, pointing to the embordered EM on the petticoat hem, "that would be Edwina Moreland!"

A chill went through Sarah. Edwina? Edwin? Winnie! Edwin's daughter Edwina nicknamed Winnie! "The child Winnie in Philippa's letters!" she whispered to Sam.

"That's right. The old girl was called Winnie. Lived till she was almost a hundred! Long gone, of course. I was a little tyke when she died. You don't forget anybody who lives to be a hundred! Why, I can remember old Winnie Moreland as clearly as if she was sitting right here next to me." He patted an empty chair seat.

Sarah looked around, half expecting to see Edwina sitting next to him. "Oh, please tell us about her."

"Well, I'm supposed to be cooking, you know. Your fish and chips can be handled back there without me. A more elaborate order comes in, I'll have to scoot back to the kitchen."

"Anything you have time for would be great," said Samuel.

"Well, let's see now. My grandad, may he rest with the angels, used to talk about old Winnie. She was an eccentric, all right. A bit strange, you might say. Her mum practically abandoned her, you see. Left her to be raised by servants. The mum went into a great depression after Winnie was born. Nowadays doctors can treat that kind of thing and control it. But in those days they didn't know what to do about it. Her way out was to take to the bottle. Ladylike, you know. Brandy, I believe it was. But alcohol all the same. Destroyed her finally." The innkeeper shook his head sadly.

"And the little girl?" asked Sarah. "Edwina. What happened to her?"

"Well, there was a father. Edwin Moreland. Showered her with everything a child could want. But he was away on business a good deal of the time. So there was no one but the mum tucked away in her room, the servants, and Winnie in the big house most of the time. Now you can't bring up a child without love. Even a puppy needs affection."

"Wasn't there anyone special who loved her?" prodded Sarah.

"I'm trying to think," said the innkeeper, scratching his forehead. "My grandad used to tell about all the tragedy that happened up there at Morelands. Mrs. Moreland's drinking wasn't the only thing. Now what was it? Been years since I thought about it."

The waitress brought their fish and chips and everyone began nibbling. Sarah was too excited to eat.

"Yes, now I recall what happened." He shook his head in a satisfied nod.

"What was that?" asked Sarah eagerly..

"Well, there was a governess. She was someone who loved that little girl. An American, like you, young lady. She and the little girl got along smashingly. The father liked her too. Maybe he liked her too well. For a time there, the three of them were rather thick. Went everywhere together. Went riding on the moors. A bit lonely on the moors. Away from prying eyes, you might say. Well, word got around anyway. The wife didn't like that one bit. Roused herself from her drunkenness to accuse the governess of stealing the family jewels. Then suddenly there was the accident. No one knew who was to blame. The governess's horse just buckled under. Went down one of those rocky crags like a leaf in the wind. Never breathed again. Not the woman. Nor the horse."

Sarah's eyes filled up. So that was how Philippa died. That was the tragic ending her mother had mentioned.

"Did the governess steal the jewels?" asked Jane.

"They never found them. No one knows what happened to the jewels," answered the innkeeper.

"I know Philippa didn't steal any jewels," said Sarah vehemently.

Sam put his arm around Sarah. "Come on," he said gently. "That happened in 1853 or 1854. That's a long, long time ago. You can't be upset over something that happened so many years ago."

"Sorry if I upset you, young lady. 'Tis a sad story. But I didn't think you'd take it so hard." The innkeeper got up guiltily and started back into the kitchen.

"Wait," said Sarah. "I'm okay. I want to hear the rest of it."

"Not much more to tell. The little girl grew up and lived a very long life. Died in about 1948. Never married and had kids like the rest of us."

"What about the father?" asked Sam.

"Well, he was broken-hearted. As was the little one. That governess must have been very special. It was obvious they both loved her very much. There was talk of foul play. Some thought the horse had been drugged. But it never was proved, you know. Edwin Moreland was a changed man after the accident. Blamed himself, I guess. He loved that child, though. She was his only joy, they said. Pity, you know. He was a handsome figure of a man in his day. My grandfather said they made quite a picture, the three of them riding the splendid Moreland horses across the moors."

The waitress came over to the innkeeper. "We have two orders of veal Parmesan at table four. They want you in the kitchen."

The innkeeper ignored the waitress and stared dreamily into the far corners of the room. "I can remember old Winnie even though I was very little. Used to come into the inn here for a spot of tea when she was in town." The innkeeper smiled proudly. "This inn has been in our family for years. But she was a solemn one, that Edwina. Like the sunshine had gone out of her life when she was little and it never came back in."

The innkeeper patted Sarah's brown curls. "But don't worry that pretty head of yours over what happened so many years ago. And I can't really swear that any of what I told you is really true. The story is only local gossip as I heard it through the years!" And off he went to prepare the veal Parmesan.

❧14❧

The Moreland Family Jewels

"Sarah dear, do eat your lunch before it gets too cold," said Aunt Emma.

"I can't help thinking how strange it all is," said Sarah. "Here we all sit, calmly eating. Yet whether we like it or not, we're all involved with our great-great-great-aunt Philippa. She came to England to visit your ancestors back in 1853. We have a portrait of her, and a chest of letters she wrote. Then someone shows up with a locket that has a copy of her portrait in it. Next, I find a doll that she made. And then the innkeeper tells us that the doll was made for Edwina Moreland, who was probably the Winnie that Philippa wrote about."

"And," added cousin Felicity, "we also learn that the governess, who just had to be Philippa, died because someone may have drugged her horse. I agree with Sarah. There has to be a reason all these things about Philippa are surfacing now."

"What do you think the reason is?" asked Jane.

"I wish I knew," said Sarah as she finally began eating her fish and chips.

"I don't think it's so strange," said Samuel. "One thing sparks another. If we hadn't needed money to fix up the house, we never would have been up in the attic searching for something to sell. We would never have discovered the letters, or at least not now. And if we hadn't started The Yankee Spirit, we never would have met the Chaneys, who brought the locket. Then," Sam went on, "when you learned that the locket came from England, Sarah, it reminded you that we hadn't seen our cousins in a long time. So you wrote to them. And here we are. In the very neighborhood where Philippa lived and worked as a governess. So it isn't totally strange that we found a doll she made for Edwin's daughter. It all makes sense to me."

"So then," said Jane, "it all started because you needed money. Maybe that code came to light because Philippa's ghost knew that and wanted to help you by leading you to something valuable. And I hate to say it, but maybe she's trying to lead you to the Moreland family jewels."

Sarah shook her head. "I just know that she wouldn't have stolen those jewels," she said dramatically. "Maybe Philippa's soul is tormented because she was wrongly accused of stealing them. Since she couldn't clear her name herself, she wants us to do it."

"Philippa's ghost! Philippa's soul! How delicious!" said Felicity with a little shudder.

"I don't really believe in ghosts," said Samuel. "I would rather think that these are all coincidences. We'll know if it all means anything if we ever figure out that darn code. Then we'll know if the nonsense poem is hiding the jewels that were never found."

"Philippa never stole anything, I just know it!" repeated Sarah. "We have to figure out her message now more than ever. We need to see if the poem holds clues to something valuable. But we also have to clear Philippa's name."

"That isn't going to be so easy. Sarah showed you the poem," Samuel said to his two cousins, "and you couldn't make heads or tails of it either."

They all sat, silently munching away on their fish and chips as they thought about the difficulties in solving the code.

"How come Philippa was working in Edwin's home? After all, she told Evangeline never to mention his name again," asked Sarah.

"That may have been pure chance. She could have applied for the job when the father was away."

"She would have known that the last name was the same," said Sarah. "She must have known he was Edwin Moreland, and here she was taking a job there. That bothers me."

"Unless," said Felicity, "she went for the job knowing full well it was Morelands. But she thought her sister in prim New England would never approve of her living in the same house with Edwin. After all, that was a pretty nervy thing to do. Even though Edwin had no real marriage with his wife, he still was married to her. Do you suppose he convinced Philippa that they should take whatever happiness they could until they were someday able to marry? Perhaps he begged her to come because the child needed her so badly. And maybe she just couldn't resist him. The innkeeper said he was very handsome!"

At that moment, the innkeeper, as if hearing his name, walked into the dining room with two portions of veal Parmesan. He carried them over to table four and then turned to Sarah.

"Young lady, there's one more thing I remembered. This might intrigue you. You see, before old Mrs. Moreland died, she accused her husband and daughter of being in collusion with the governess and knowing where the jewels were. Since no one ever saw those jewels, it was generally thought that after the governess died, Edwina may have hidden them. But in her will Edwina left everything to an orphanage and there was no mention of jewels. There was an estate sale of all the valuables, and the jewels never turned up there either. So apparently old Winnie really didn't have them. Maybe the governess did steal them. In any case, young lady, as far I know the jewels have never turned up. I thought you might like to ponder that little mystery." He went back into the kitchen.

"I hate to say it, Sarah, but you have to face the fact that Philippa may have stolen them," said Jane.

"Philippa was not a thief. I keep telling you that!" Sarah was annoyed at Jane for even suggesting such a thing. "You can tell in a minute that she was a completely good and honest person just by looking at her portrait."

"Wouldn't it be something if the Moreland jewels are really what the code is hiding?" said Sam.

"And we're the ones destined to find them," said Sarah. "That's why all this has happened! You said it all started with our need for money, Sam! And now Mom needs money to renovate the barn!"

"Oh, this is all so exciting," said Felicity. "Philippa is trying to reach out to you as best she can. She wants to help you locate the jewels, to provide you with a treasure for your bed and breakfast business, and incidentally, to clear her name. Her spirit won't rest until you find them."

"If Evangeline ever found the jewels," Jane added,

"she may have been too proud to take them. Or she may have taken what she needed and left the rest hidden."

"Or she could have forgotten her childhood code and never figured out where they were in the first place," said Sam.

"Maybe Evangeline was too upset about her husband's death, and then Philippa's death right after that, to even think about the code," said Sarah.

"We could ponder the possibilities forever. Unless you can read that coded message you'll never know," said Jane, adding a little more ketchup to her chips.

"*I'll* figure out that code," said Sarah. "You wait and see!"

❧15❧

Morelands

After lunch the four young people begged Aunt Emma to let them visit the home that had once belonged to Edwin Moreland.

The innkeeper cheerfully gave them directions to Morelands. "Fortunate thing for this town that the new people are putting the old place back in good shape. I expect many tourists will be attracted to it. And of course tourists need to eat, you know!"

They drove through the town and easily found the road leading up to the impressive iron gates mentioned by the innkeeper. Since the gates were wide open, they felt free to enter.

"Aunt Emma, could I get out and walk?" Sarah asked, as Jane guided the car through a parklike area on a tree-lined road. "I want to see the place slowly, just as Philippa saw it. I'll meet you up at the house."

Felicity got out of the car too. Linking her arm through Sarah's, she said, "I'd like to go with you. Do you mind?"

"Of course not. In fact I'm happy that you don't think me peculiar. But as we started to drive in here I had the weirdest feeling. I feel as though I'm traveling back in time."

"I certainly don't think you're peculiar," answered Felicity. "I'm also fascinated with Philippa's story. I know I don't feel quite as strongly as you do about her. Why, when Jane suggested that Philippa might have stolen the jewels, I thought you'd slap her!"

"I was annoyed, a little. It's just that I feel I know Philippa so well and I don't believe she could have stolen anything."

"Sarah, when you talk about her, your eyes get a sort of out-of-this-world look. It's almost as though . . . now this may sound silly, but it's almost as though the spirit of Philippa has invaded you!"

"Maybe it has," sighed Sarah. "When I put on her dress I had the strangest feeling that I was Philippa. Even my dog didn't recognize me!"

Felicity smiled. "Animals have a special sense about these things."

They walked on in silence, each thinking her own thoughts.

"Felicity," said Sarah, staring at the green fields

surrounding the road, "this is my first trip to England. So I can't possibly have ever seen this place, but . . . I have the strangest feeling that I've been here before."

"Maybe you've read so much about Philippa and her travels that you feel you've actually experienced everything with her. That sometimes happens."

Sarah had no time to respond. Having rounded a curve in the tree-lined road, the two cousins came suddenly upon a wonderful brick manorhouse. Although obviously in need of repair, it was still beautiful with its graceful outlines silhouetted majestically against the sky.

A broad terrace overlooked two curved staircases that ended just a few feet from a round pool with a fountain in the center. A small stone angel, its wings broken off, lay in a crumbling heap in the center of the fountain.

"Pity," Sarah said in an unnaturally soft voice. "That angel once stood on tiptoe right in the center of that fountain. The water tumbled down all around it."

"Why, Sarah, you sound as though you've seen that angel before," said Jane, laughing at her.

The staircase had many broken treads and the balustrade surrounding the terrace was hanging loose in several places. It didn't matter at all. The impression was still one of grand style.

"It must have been strange for Philippa to be living here," said Sarah. "It was so different from the life she knew back in Connecticut!"

The others were getting out of the car and looking around when the front door of the manorhouse opened. A young woman, incongruously dressed in jeans and sneakers in the midst of all this former elegance, smiled at them.

"Hello! I'm Betsy Cogswell. My husband and I are the owners. Can I help you?"

Aunt Emma explained that they were curious to see the place a relative of theirs had lived in many generations ago. She introduced the four young people, who shook hands politely with Mrs. Cogswell.

"We're in the process of modernizing and repairing. We've been at it for over a year. We've cleared out masses of old junk that had accumulated through the years. So the place is a bit of a mess, but would you like to see the inside?"

Would they! Sarah dashed up the moss-covered stone steps and waited impatiently for the others to follow. Mrs. Cogswell led them into the cool interior of a large, circular front hall. An enormous stone fireplace was centered in one wall of the room. Huge portraits in heavy gold frames hung all around them.

Betsy Cogswell waved her hand nonchalantly around the walls. "Ready-made ancestors! Not one is ours. We inherited them when we bought the house. We've adopted them for our own, although we don't even know exactly who they are."

Sarah, in a kind of dreamy trance, walked past several portraits to stand in front of a large painting of a handsome man in riding clothes. "Edwin Moreland! I'd know him anywhere." She walked over to the next painting and gasped in astonishment. "Why, it's Philippa!" she cried. "Samuel, come here . . . look at this . . . it's Philippa!"

Betsy Cogswell was astounded. Who were these strangers who could identify the old portraits? Looking at Sarah closely, she couldn't help but notice her strong resemblance to the young woman in the portrait. "Who are you? How do you know all this?" she finally asked.

Aunt Emma explained that Sarah had discovered a chest of letters from her great-great-great-aunt that described her stay here.

"But Philippa wasn't a relative of the Morelands," said Jane. "She was only a governess in the house. How come they had a portrait of her here?"

"I didn't know she was the governess," answered Mrs. Cogswell. "I only know that the last member of the family, Edwina Moreland, commissioned this painting back in the 1930s. See, here's the date," she said, pointing to the corner of the painting. They all could clearly see the date, 1933, painted with a flourish under the artist's signature. "The artist copied it from a miniature in a locket that I can't show you, because it's been sold. I thought perhaps it was of her mother." Mrs. Cogswell walked over to another painting. "We think from the style of the dress and the date that this must be a portrait of Edwina as a child," she said, pointing to a picture of a five-year-old girl holding a doll.

Sarah let out a shriek. "Look, Sam, look at this!"

The child in the painting was holding her doll, the doll Philippa had made for her, the very doll Sarah had purchased that morning. "I have it right here!" she said as she unwrapped the tissue-paper package she was holding.

"See, Aunt Emma," she exclaimed triumphantly, holding up the doll alongside the one in the portrait. "I knew it was Philippa's doll. I knew it!"

Betsy Cogswell laughed. "You must have bought that in town. I brought it down only last week. We've been selling things off all this past year to pay bills. We figure modern bathrooms and a good kitchen are much more important to us than things like dolls and lockets."

"That was the locket that Mrs. Chaney brought to our house! Mrs. Cogswell, we have a painting of that same person back in America. It's our great-great-great-aunt Philippa!" said Samuel.

"And," explained Jane, "we believe the painting of Philippa is hanging there with the rest of the family members because to Edwina Moreland, Philippa was more dear to her than her own mother."

"Edwin Moreland must have loved Philippa too," said Mrs. Cogswell. "In a closet next to what we understand was his bedroom, there was a kind of shrine. The locket was hung on the wall and two beautiful silver candlesticks were placed on either side of it. A little rug in front was all worn out, as if someone had knelt there often. Of course we had to take it all down when we moved in last February."

Sarah turned to Sam. "February! Wasn't it about then that I began to dream about Philippa?"

"Yup. It was February. How could I forget! It was right after . . . right after . . . Dad died. That's when we discovered the chest of letters. It's all such a . . . such a fantastic set of coincidences."

"Or," said Felicity solemnly, "Philippa's spirit was set free when Mrs. Cogswell took down the little shrine and sold the locket."

"Don't be ridiculous, Felicity," said the practical Aunt Emma. "I've listened to you four talking about ghosts and spirits long enough. You don't really believe in such things as spirits!"

"I don't know what to believe," answered Felicity. "But Sarah is certainly being pushed by someone or something to discover all these things about Philippa. It's getting pretty hard to ignore."

"Gracious me," said Mrs. Cogswell. "What an extraordinary tale you are telling. What can it all mean?"

Aunt Emma wanted to change the subject. "Can we see more of the house?" she asked.

"With pleasure," said Mrs. Cogswell, leading the way.

For Sarah, Morelands seemed more dreamlike than real. She could almost hear the rustle of Philippa's full-skirted dress as she walked along from room to room. At the nursery on the top floor, she was oddly at home as she sat down on one of the low built-in seats under the window. "Philippa sat here when she was teaching Winnie to embroider." She looked out of the window, half expecting to see Edwin riding through the fields below.

Aunt Emma put her arm around Sarah's shoulders. "Sarah's mother warned me that Sarah tends to be a bit dramatic," she said to Mrs. Cogswell. "And my Felicity is the same way. These two are quite a pair!"

Outside the nursery, Sarah turned to a small door on the right. "Philippa's bedroom," she said as if there were no question about it.

"Why, yes, my dear, it was a small bedroom. And probably the governess did sleep there," said Betsy Cogswell, opening the door to a bare little room with a small window overlooking the back terrace.

The others moved on, but Sarah went straight to the window. In a matter of seconds she was tracing her finger over a small PB etched in the corner of one of the panes. "I knew you were here, Philippa. As always, you left your mark," she whispered.

She heard her aunt call her, but she was unable to move. She had never felt so close to Philippa before. Not even in her own bedroom at home. Suddenly she pulled back in surprise and shock. There, filling the entire window, was Philippa's face!

"Sarah, uncover what I have in mind," whispered Philippa, exactly as she had in the past. And then, before Sarah could say a word, the face vanished.

Samuel stood at the door. "What are you doing,

Sarah? We're all going downstairs. Aunt Emma was wondering where you were. What's the matter?" he asked as he saw his sister's astonished look.

Sarah shook her head. "Nothing. Nothing at all," she said as she followed Sam downstairs. She saw no point in telling him about Philippa's face. Maybe it was only her imagination after all. Maybe the strong vibrations she was getting about Philippa were making her see things that weren't really there.

As they got into the car, thanking Mrs. Cogswell for the tour, Samuel had one more question to ask. "I hope you won't think me too nosy, Mrs. Cogswell. But by any chance when you were clearing out the house, did you come upon the Moreland family jewels? The innkeeper in town said that Edwina Moreland may have hidden them here."

"That was a rumor we heard, too. Oh, how I wish we had discovered them! We certainly could have used the money they would have brought. Unfortunately, we came upon nothing in the way of jewels other than the locket that friend of yours bought. We've gone over the whole place inch by inch by now, and if there were jewels hidden anywhere, we would have found them."

Sarah managed to return to her normal self and waved good-bye to Mrs. Cogswell with the others. "It's clearer than ever," she thought. "Philippa needs me to find those jewels!"

❧16❧

Home Again

The next days were filled with wonderful trips in the nearby countryside. They drove down to Land's End, the very last tip of land on the British Isles. To Sarah and Samuel, it seemed truly to be the edge of the world. It was hard to imagine that somewhere, curving beyond their vision, lay America and home. While Sarah knew that she and Sam were only six or seven hours away from home by plane, she could imagine how Philippa felt, so far from home in the days of slow ships that took weeks to cross the Atlantic.

They visited the harbor at Plymouth, where they felt the connecting link between England and America as they realized that this was where Sir Francis Drake, the Pilgrim fathers, and Captain John Cook set sail.

They went bathing in the sea at one of the sandy beach resorts along the coast, and they walked down the steepest street they had ever seen in the pretty little town of Clovelly, where fishing boats huddled below in the harbor. They were fascinated to learn that this was the part of the country where King Arthur was said to have fought his battles. They loved climbing around the romantic ruins of what was supposed to be his birthplace at Tintagel castle.

And every place they visited, Sarah wondered whether Philippa had been there in the faraway past. She could just imagine her sitting and sketching as she tried to record everything she saw for her sister Evangeline.

Hiking through the open fields called moors, they saw mysterious stone burial grounds and sacred circles from prehistoric times. In the moody atmosphere surrounding these dark stones, Sarah could feel Philippa's spirit close by, hovering around them along with the pixies and giants and demons that were still supposed to hop about the area.

They ate the famous Devon cream, which was so thick it wouldn't pour. Their hands were stained red with the fresh strawberries they picked in the fields. They picnicked on Cornish pasties at the romantic ruins of a castle in Dorset. But no matter what they did, Sarah's thoughts were never far from Philippa.

And then, after the fastest two weeks they had ever experienced, it was time for Sarah and Samuel to return to America. Everyone was saddened at the thought. It had been a wonderful vacation. Not only had they enjoyed themselves, but Sarah felt that she had learned a great deal about Philippa. The cousins promised to write and visit. Aunt Emma invited Sarah and Samuel to come back whenever they cared to.

Sarah, fearful that her luggage might get lost, carried her doll with her onto the airplane. Felicity had given her a box and some cloth to wrap it in. "After all," laughed her cousin, "I wouldn't want you to look like a huge five-year-old carrying your dolly in your arms!"

Sarah kept the box right beside her for the seven and a half hours they were in the air. Mrs. Bingham met them at the airport, where they had a happy reunion full of hugs and chatter. Sarah, impatient to show her mother her treasured purchase, couldn't resist unwrapping the package right there in the middle of the airport.

Mrs. Bingham was stunned as she recognized the doll from the portrait in their living room. When she recovered herself, she said, "How fantastic that you found it! It does look exactly like the doll in the painting and it's wonderful for us to have it. But, Sarah, I was hoping that you would get a rest from Philippa!"

"Oh Mom, wait till we tell you about Morelands and the paintings we saw and what an innkeeper told us about Edwina Moreland, who was Edwin's daughter and the Winnie in the letters. You're going to feel just as I do about her. Even Sam has come to believe that there is something special about all this. Right, Sam?"

Samuel nodded, but Mrs. Bingham quickly held up her hands and said, "We've plenty of time for all that. We should be getting out of the airport and on our way home before the heavy traffic starts."

"How are things back at The Yankee Spirit?" asked Sam as they walked to the parking lot.

Mrs. Bingham smiled as she said, "You wouldn't believe how busy we were! And everyone who comes to stay says they'll be back! There was another write-up in a magazine about us. We've been called 'one of the most charming bed and breakfasts in New England'! How proud Dad would have been! We've created a fine business for ourselves. Now our only problem is to save enough money for a new roof. Lucky for you two that the roof problems developed after you left. I never would have been able to spare the airfare before. We had some heavy rainstorms over these past two weeks and we've had some bad leaks. They're patched up for now, but the roofer tells me it won't be long before we have to replace the old roof. And that's an expensive job. I haven't yet figured out what we're going to do about it."

Sarah hugged her mother again. "Oh, Mom, don't worry. Something good will happen. I just know it will. Maybe we'll break the code and find Philippa's treasure." Stashing her carry-on bag in the car, she climbed in after it.

Mrs. Bingham started the motor. "I wouldn't count on Philippa so much, Sarah. Why, you seem to be more involved with her now than before you went away. And to think I hoped you'd get away from thinking about her. By the way," she said, happy to change the subject, "the Chaneys are coming next month to see the fall colors."

"With Martha and John?" asked Samuel.

"Of course the children are coming too," answered Mrs. Bingham. She noticed that both Sarah and Samuel blushed as she said, "I didn't know you were so interested in John and Martha."

"Sam's been writing to Martha," said Sarah casually.

"As if you weren't busy writing to John all summer," said Sam.

"School starts in two weeks," said Sarah quickly. "I guess we'll have a lot of work to do to fill up the freezer again with muffins. And I want to try making some scones. We had them at Aunt Emma's at tea time every day. Are they ever good!"

"I'll help you, Sarah," said Sam. "Since the wood supply wasn't used over the summer, I'm still way ahead with the chopping."

"There's a pile of mail back home for you two. If you answer it all, you can spend a few days just doing that," said Mrs. Bingham. "And we'll have to go shopping for some school clothes. You both look as though you grew a few inches over the summer."

As they turned onto the highway leading to Connecticut, Sarah turned to Sam. "I hope there's a letter from John. He promised to work on the code over the summer. Maybe he figured it out! Wouldn't that be the greatest homecoming present!"

❧17❧

Back to
the Old Routine

It was great to be home. Bingo jumped all over them squealing happily and smearing wet kisses on them. As much as Sarah and Sam had enjoyed their trip, there was nothing quite like the feeling of stepping once again into the warmth and familiarity of home. There was a comforting sense of belonging that no other place on earth could give them. Perhaps it took being away from home to fully appreciate it.

The first thing Sarah did was sort through the mail. Putting aside the mail-order catalogues, she finally found what she wanted. Two letters from John Chaney!

Without stopping to unpack or put away her things, she settled into the rocking chair near the living room fireplace and ripped open the envelopes. She surprised even herself with the eagerness she felt at hearing from the young man she had seen for only two days.

John had received one of her postcards from England. He was pleased that she was enjoying herself. He had a job teaching softball to eight-year-old boys and girls in one of the New York City parks. He was happy that he was going to see her again in October. He hoped they would get along as well as they had before. No mention of the code in either letter.

Sarah was disappointed. "He's forgotten all about it," she said to Sam. Unwrapping the doll, she carefully set her on the mantlepiece near the painting of Philippa. "There," she said, spreading out the skirt of the doll's calico dress. "You once belonged to Edwina, but now that she's gone, you really belong right here next to the person who created you!" Sarah looked up at the painting. She could almost imagine a faint smile on Philippa's solemn face as she said, "I bet you're pleased to have her back too!"

Sarah and Sam yawned sleepily all through dinner. Mrs. Bingham told them that they were feeling jet lag. It was really five hours later for them, according to the time in England that they had become accustomed to. "Go to sleep," she said. "I'll clear up the dishes."

Tired as she was, Sarah couldn't resist getting out

the little chest of letters after she had unpacked. Now, after actually seeing Morelands and the Devon countryside, she could visualize what Philippa was writing about. Reading drowsily through the familiar letters, she could almost imagine she heard the soft voice she had come to associate with Philippa.

When she came to the nonsense poem, she shook her head sadly. No matter how many times she read it, it still made no sense to her. Jane and Felicity hadn't been any help either. "I guess I'm too tired now. I thought perhaps after so many days away I would have some new ideas," she sighed. Putting the letters down, she walked over to the window and idly rubbed the etched PB with her finger. "Philippa," she yawned, "I need your help."

Suddenly the room went dark. The overhead light was snuffed out! Sarah turned to see if Sam or her mother had flipped it off. But no one else was in the room. The entire house was silent.

"The bulb must have blown," she said aloud, hoping that her own voice would calm the sudden fluttering of her heart.

What a moment to be in the darkness! Was Philippa responsible? She pulled her flashlight out of the top drawer of the table near her bed and nervously put the letters away. As she tucked the last one into the chest, she heard a rustling sound. Goose bumps crowded onto her skin. Holding her breath, Sarah flashed her light into the corners of her room. Empty! She let out her breath with relief. There was no one there! But something odd was happening.

A pinpoint of light was swirling in the center of the room! Was she imagining it? The tiny round shape seemed to be growing larger and larger until it was the size of a person's head. It *was* a head. Good heavens! It was Philippa's face again, looking straight at her with a sad smile.

"Be patient, Sarah," said Philippa, before she quickly faded away to nothingness.

This all took place in a fraction of a second. Sarah thought that perhaps she had dozed off and dreamt the whole thing. But it seemed so real! And the room was still in darkness!

She ran into Samuel's room and climbed onto the end of his bed. Sam had dozed off while reading one of the bicycle magazines he had gotten in the mail. "Sam," said Sarah, waking him. "Philippa was back. And my light went out just before she appeared. It was like an omen. She told me to be patient and then she disappeared. Do you believe me? Or am I going crazy?"

Sam yawned as he put away his magazine. "I don't know what to believe any more. I don't think you're crazy. I do think you are very tired. We've had a long trip. You could have dozed off like I just did and imagined you heard Philippa say whatever you wanted to hear. Go to sleep. I'm too tired to figure it out. We'll talk about it in the morning."

Sarah went back to her room and tried switching on her light. It still didn't work. "I guess it really did blow out. But what a weird coincidence! I'll change the bulb in the morning."

The next days were spent busily getting things back to normal for the two travelers. Between helping out at The Yankee Spirit, berry picking, baking, shopping, and greeting their friends down at the lake, there was little time for Philippa or the code.

"It's hard to believe," said Sam one morning as he cleared away the breakfast dishes, "but we've been home for a month already. It almost feels as if we've never been away!"

"Oh, I know we've been away," said Sarah, glancing up at the mantle where the little doll sat serenely watching all that went on in the household. "And I'm well aware that it is precisely one month, because tomorrow is Saturday, the day the Chaneys arrive."

"Counting the days, are you?" asked Samuel with a smile.

"Look who's talking!" said Sarah. "I suppose you're not interested in seeing Martha!"

"Okay, okay, I admit it," said Sam, running outside before Sarah could see the pink tinge flushing over his face.

Saturday morning Sarah tried on three shirts before she was satisfied with the way she looked. Passing her room, Mrs. Bingham smiled as she realized that this was the first time she had ever seen Sarah so conscious of what she was wearing. "At least she's not totally preoccupied with Philippa," she said to herself.

What Mrs. Bingham didn't know was that Sarah was not only looking forward to seeing her new friend but was counting on him to help her solve the code. She was determined to spend the entire weekend at it, if necessary.

❦18❧

Codes and Ciphers

Samuel, out on the lawn brushing Bingo's sleek black coat, was the first to hear the crunch of car wheels on the gravel of the parking area.

"They're here, Sarah, they're here," he yelled. He and Bingo almost fell over each other as they ran to greet the Chaneys. After a few shy greetings Sam and John and Martha began talking as if they had seen each other only the day before.

John was removing two bicycles from a rack on top of the car when Sarah stepped outside.

"Hello, Sarah," said Mrs. Chaney. "How was England?"

"Fabulous. Everything you said it would be. We loved it!"

"Find any lockets?" asked Mr. Chaney with a mischievous smile.

"Not exactly, but close," said Sarah, laughing and turning to John, leaving Mr. Chaney to wonder what she meant.

"You've brought your bikes! That's great." She loved the idea of going on a long bike ride with John and Martha, but it occurred to her that John might have put aside all thought of solving the code.

"We've got good roads for riding around here," said Sam, giving John a hand with the bikes. "And the weather is supposed to be great all weekend."

"Well," said John. "There's nothing I'd like better than a long bike trip, but I had another idea too. Is there a library around here?"

"A library? Of course! But why? Do you have homework to do?" asked a clearly disappointed Sam.

"I really brought the bikes so we could pedal over to a library and see if there's a book on deciphering codes."

"What a great idea!" exclaimed Sarah, wondering why she herself had never thought of seeking help from the library. "But we don't all have to go to the library," she added, seeing Sam's gloomy face. "I can go with John, and you two can go off anywhere you like and we'll meet back here."

"That's fine with me," said Martha.

"First help us unload the rest of this luggage, and

then you two are on your own," said Mr. Chaney. He handed her a small suitcase.

"Give me five minutes to change my clothes," said Martha, running into the house with the suitcase.

"You've got the same rooms you had last time you were here," Mrs. Bingham called after her as she greeted the Chaneys.

"I can't tell you how happy we all are to be back," said Mrs. Chaney. "It's like returning to the old homestead!"

"I hope you don't mind that we've adopted your family home for the one we never had," Mr. Chaney said, laughing.

"I'm happy you feel so comfortable here," said Mrs. Bingham. "That's what we hoped would happen."

After tying her knapsack onto the back of her bike, Sarah set out for the library with John. The crisp autumn morning was perfection. Foliage of splashy reds and bright yellows surrounded the two bike riders with an almost unbelievable intensity of color. Occasional leaves floated down from the trees like bright butterflies in the wind.

"It's great to see you again," said John shyly.

"I'm glad you came back, too," answered Sarah.

"You're so lucky," said John, as he admired the colorful landscape. "You get to see the seasons changing. In the city, unless you go to the park, the main difference in the seasons is the temperature. Where we live there are only a few trees. And those are set in the sidewalks and surrounded by big buildings with only a little piece of sky over them. They never seem·to turn colors as bright as these."

"I guess my favorite season is this time of year," said Sarah, pedaling beside John. "No matter how many times I've seen the fall colors, each year they always seem to come as a shock."

"How far is the library?" asked John, struggling up one of Connecticut's many hills.

"Tired already?" Sarah laughed as she easily rode on ahead of him. "C'mon, city slicker, you'll make it. It's only three miles!"

The three miles actually were covered very quickly. They parked their bikes in front of an ornate Victorian building that was the town library. Sarah admitted to John that she should have thought of going to the library sooner. She hadn't realized there were books on codes.

"There are books on everything," said John. "But wait before you congratulate me for having a good idea. Let's see what we come up with—it's worth a try. I could have gone to the library in the city, but I thought it would be more fun to go with you."

"I'm glad you waited for me," said Sarah as she pushed open the heavy carved door.

While the outside of the library was built of old-fashioned, deeply carved stone, the inside was a completely modern and sleek surprise. "It was just redone," whispered Sarah proudly as they headed for the librarian's desk.

"Mrs. Wolinsky, this is my friend from New York, John Chaney," she said as the librarian greeted her familiarly. "We're looking for some information on breaking codes. Do you think there's anything here to help us?"

"Codes? You mean computer codes?" asked Mrs. Wolinsky.

Sarah and John both laughed. "Computers weren't invented when this code was written," said Sarah.

"You see," explained John, "we've got a nonsense poem we think may hold a coded message, and we need help in figuring it out."

Mrs. Wolinsky was flipping through a huge alphabetical index of all the subjects that books had been written about. She was looking for anything that might refer to codes. "Hmmmm," she hummed as her finger traveled down the pages. "Here it is. 'Codes!' Oh, dear, it says, 'See ciphers.' " She turned to look up "ciphers."

There was apparently quite a list of books on ciphers, but none of them were in this library. Mrs. Wolinsky's pencil tapped against the desktop as if it had a nervous tic. She hated to disappoint anyone. "I'm afraid, Sarah, if you want to see any of these books, you'll have to go to the main library in Hartford."

"We certainly can't bicycle there," said Sarah mournfully.

Mrs. Wolinsky suddenly had another thought. "You could try the *Encyclopaedia Britannica* and see what they have."

In a few minutes John was thumbing through the encyclopedia. "Who would have thought there were so many subjects beginning with *co*!" he complained. Suddenly Sarah shouted, "Look! Here's something! There's a whole column on codes!"

They both read through the column as quickly as they could. While it was interesting enough, it was really a history of codes. Unfortunately, there was no magic formula to help them solve their code.

They were about to leave when Mrs. Wolinsky stopped them. "You could try the children's library, you know. There just might be something there."

So Sarah and John trotted over to the children's room and put the same question to the young librarian who was busy tidying up a low table of books.

"Codes! Let me think for a moment. Yes, I seem to remember one. We do have a book on codes and ciphers, I'm sure of it. I haven't seen it in a while. Maybe it's out. Let me look." She searched one shelf after another, while John and Sarah waited hopefully.

Just as she was about to give up, she suddenly pulled out a slim paperbacked book. Waving it in triumph the librarian said gleefully, "I knew it! It just had to be here. It's not my most popular book, after all."

❧19❧

The Iron Box

The little book was called *The Code and Cipher Book*. It described more than twenty-five ways to write secret messages. It described methods for writing in invisible ink, and it had information about famous codes in history. Most important of all, there was a chapter on decoding or breaking codes.

Sarah pulled out Philippa's poem and some pencils and paper. Settling themselves comfortably at a quiet table near the window, she and John held the book open between them. She liked the feeling of working with John.

Together they learned that there are codes and there are ciphers. In a code, a real word has another word or symbol to stand for it. In a cipher, letters rather than words are changed.

"I'm not sure what we're dealing with," said John.

"We'll just try all the methods the book gives until we find one that makes sense," said Sarah. "Code or cipher, as long as it works!"

Chapter by chapter they followed instructions. They transposed letters. They substituted letters. They tried reading the poem backwards. They changed the spacing between the letters. They tried every third letter, every fourth letter; they tried something called the Ancient Ogum Cipher; they worked on rearranging the alphabet.

"Nothing seems to work," Sarah said in a discouraged voice after an hour.

"I'm not giving up yet," said John as he tried still another arrangement of letters described in the book.

Sarah, dejected by now, began doodling on the copy of the poem in front of her. With a red pencil she mindlessly but elaborately decorated the first letter of each line of the poem.

Suddenly she shrieked, "Look, John, look at this!"

"*Ssshhh,*" John said quickly, smiling at the librarian apologetically when she glanced with disapproval at them.

"But look at this! It's as plain as the nose on your face!"

John stared at the nonsense poem. He saw exactly

what he had always seen except for the decorated letters. He read:

S tickety wickety seventeen nickety
T odel podel about face pickety
O nkety ponkety hobbledy wonkety
N ohso wohso yeaso donkety
E ach to his own.

W ickety stickety seventeen nickety
A ddle paddle about face pickety
L ohso wohso yeaso donkety
L ohso wohso yeaso donkety

N ever to seek means never to find
E vie uncover what I have in mind.

"See," said Sarah, grinning happily. "It's all clear. We've broken the code!"

"Oh, my gosh! Of course! I see it now. It's obvious. Why didn't I see it before?"

"Why didn't I ever think to read down? STONE WALL NE! The first letter of each line makes STONE WALL NE when you read down! It makes perfect sense. NE is obviously North East. And I know exactly what wall that is!" exclaimed Sarah.

"The real words like 'seventeen' and 'about face' must actually refer to a part of the wall," said John.

"Then what are we waiting for? Let's go!"

After thanking the startled librarian profusely, they returned the little book and gleefully unlocked their bikes. The red and gold leaves of autumn danced around them merrily as if congratulating them as they rode back to the house.

Sam and Martha had returned a few minutes earlier. They were resting in the garden behind the house when Sarah and John burst in on them.

"We solved it! It was a code after all. See!" and Sarah spread out the decorated poem in front of them.

"Of course!" said Martha, seeing it right away. "How simple!"

"Well," said Sam. "Makes me feel pretty stupid not to have figured it out sooner!"

Sarah pointed to the stone wall enclosing a field on their left. "That's the most northerly wall and it runs east–west. It has to be the one!"

Sam ran into the toolshed and came back with a crowbar. "This might come in handy," he said.

"Let's go!" said Sarah. "I can hardly stand the suspense!" The four young people started running across the field just as Mr. and Mrs. Chaney emerged from the house. "My goodness, they certainly keep busy," said Mrs. Chaney. "What kind of game do you suppose they're playing?"

"I never heard of a game that uses a crowbar," said Mr. Chaney. "But they are four sensible youngsters, so I'm not going to waste any more time thinking about them. It's a beautiful day. Let's go for a walk and enjoy the fall colors."

Mrs. Bingham happened to look out the living room window. Curious about what was going on in the field, she watched as the four youngsters lined up at the corner of the northernmost wall on the property. She saw Sarah, arms outstretched for balance, walk along the top of the wall as carefully as if she were on a tightrope. The others solemnly watched with their heads bobbing up and down as if they were chanting or counting. Briefly she wondered what they were up to. Some new game, she thought idly as she went back to the article she had been working on all morning.

" . . . fourteen, fifteen, sixteen, seventeen." Sarah came to a full stop, turned about face and said, "Right here! If my paces were the same as Philippa's, then this is the spot."

The other three youngsters scrambled to the top of the stone wall. Fitted together solidly by the long-dead farmers who had cleared these fields over a century ago, the wall of mossy gray stones was still in pretty good shape.

The four of them studied the large flat rocks that formed the top layer of the wall. Right where Sarah had stopped, there was an almost perfectly round stone, thinner than the others, surrounded by a circle of several smaller stones.

"A woman alone might have been able to handle that one. The others all look so heavy," said Martha.

Sam and John removed all the smaller stones first. Then they lifted the large round stone so that Sarah could peek underneath it.

"There's a deep hollow space below," she reported. "It's dark down there so I can't really see very well."

"Just the place for something to be hidden in," said Martha, rubbing her hands together excitedly. "You'll have to remove that stone entirely so we can really get a good look."

The two boys heaved the stone over to one side. The deep hollow in the rock wall was now exposed.

Sarah and Martha were bending over the hollow when suddenly a long black snake slithered out. Martha screamed. She fell back, knocking Sarah down too.

Brushing herself off, Sarah couldn't help laughing when she saw Martha's terrified face as she scrambled to the ground below. "The snake is more afraid of you than you are of it. And it's not dangerous. It's only a garter snake!"

"Well, I'm not going up there again," said Martha. "I hate snakes!"

Sam, meanwhile, was poking into the hollow with the crowbar. "There's something flat down there, but it could be just another stone." Lying on his stomach, he pushed aside some small, loose stones down in the hollow space. He felt something too smooth to be a stone. It had sharp corners!

"I think . . . I have something!" He worked his

hands around whatever it was and pulled it up. Proudly he placed a small iron box on top of the wall!

"Oh, my!" exclaimed Martha from below. "There really is a treasure!"

Sarah stared at the box. "Would you believe it? That box has been sitting here all this time, right under our noses. Evangeline never found it!"

"Maybe Evangeline couldn't remember their code," said Sam. "Anyway, let's open it and see if there really is anything valuable inside. It would be some joke if this is just an empty box!" He carried it down from the wall so that Martha could see too.

Mrs. Bingham glanced out the window again. She saw that the four young people were now sitting in a circle near the stone wall. Satisfied that they seemed to be deeply involved in whatever they were doing, she went back to her work.

❧20❧

Edwin Moreland's Gift

The lid was so rusted it wouldn't budge. Sam poked and pushed. He banged and pried. Nothing happened.

"I can't stand the suspense," cried Sarah. "We've got to get that box open!"

Suddenly Sam stopped prying at the box and turned to his sister. "Now Sarah, don't get your hopes up. This box may have nothing in it at all. Be prepared for a disappointment."

"Yes," said Sarah, "but then again it may have a treasure inside and Philippa's messages will have been right, and . . . and . . . oh, hurry. Let's not talk, let's get it open!"

"We may have to get a saw to cut through all this rust," said John as he tried working on the box. Like

Sam, he poked and pushed. He banged and pried. Then, when he was just about to give up, the lid sprang open!

"You did it!" cried Sarah admiringly.

"I loosened it for him," muttered Sam.

"There is something inside! Look!" Sarah lifted out a small packet wrapped in what had once been soft brown leather. It was in such a state of decay that it powdered away in her hands, revealing another wrapping of cloth. Sarah pulled off her sweater and spread it out on the ground so that she could carefully lay the cloth-wrapped package on top of it. The others watched her every move breathlessly.

"It's wrapped like a mummy," said Martha as Sarah slowly unwound the cloth. The top layer was brown with age, but as she uncovered the lower layers, several smaller packets appeared, each wrapped in . . . gray and pink calico!

"The same material the doll's dress is made of!" shrieked Sarah. "This is Philippa's box, for sure!"

"Oh, it's so exciting," cried Martha. "Hurry!"

By now Sarah had unraveled the largest packet.

"I don't believe it!" shouted Sam as he saw what Sarah was lifting out of the packet.

"Good heavens!" squealed Martha.

"Well, I'll be darned!" exclaimed John.

Sarah seemed to have lost her voice altogether. Wide-eyed with awe, she found herself holding, between two shaky fingers . . . a magnificent diamond and emerald necklace! Its green and clear stones twinkled in the sunlight as if blinking from the sudden exposure to daylight.

"The Moreland family jewels!" said Sarah.

"So Philippa did steal them, after all," said Sam.

"I refuse to believe she stole them. There must be an explanation as to how she came to have them!" Sarah exclaimed.

She unwrapped a smaller packet. With nervous fingers she pulled out a diamond and emerald bracelet that matched the necklace. Quickly she reached for another packet. By now she was almost ripping off the cloth wrapping to reveal an incredibly beautiful . . . diamond tiara. Impulsively she popped it on her head. The diamonds sparkled merrily among her brown curls.

"You look like a queen!" squealed Martha.

There was one packet left. It was too much for Sarah. she handed it to Samuel. "I can't! You open it. I'm too jittery."

Sam carefully unwound the cloth. When he held up a gold locket, just like the one in the painting and the one Mrs. Chaney had bought, Sarah very nearly fainted.

"I can't believe it! Another locket! Open it," she exclaimed as the diamond tiara wobbled comically on her head.

"Do you suppose it's another portrait of Philippa?" asked Martha as Sam pushed the little spring on the cover of the locket.

Their heads together over the locket in Sam's hand, the four young people were stunned and speechless. There in front of them, exposed to the light of day for the first time in over a hundred and fifty years, was another portrait. Only this wasn't a portrait of Philippa. It was of a handsome gentleman with light brown curly hair!

Sarah was the first to find her voice. "Edwin Moreland! That's him! It's the same face we saw at Morelands in the portrait of the man in riding clothes." She sat dumbly staring at the glittering pile of extravagant jewels on her sweater.

"They're so big and fancy they almost look like fakes," said Sam. "If they're real they must be worth a fortune!"

"They're real, all right!" said Sarah. "I can't wait to show Mom." She began folding the cloth that had wrapped the packets. She was about to put them back in the iron box when she suddenly exclaimed, "Look, there's a letter at the bottom of the box!"

"Another letter from Philippa?" asked Sam.

Sarah shook her head. "This is not from Philippa." She began reading aloud.

"My dearest Philippa,
These jewels rightfully belong to the beloved of the master of Morelands. That, my sweet darling, means you.
Let me explain what I couldn't say in person.

I tried to be a good husband to my poor demented wife. She was never quite stable in her mind, but things progressed for the worse after the child was born. She became a recluse, rejecting me and the child completely. She lived in her rooms, alone and in silence with only a few servants whom she allowed to attend her. I did not have the heart to confine her to an institution. The doctors now tell me that considering the fragile state of her health, she cannot live too long. Death would be a blessed relief for her.

When the situation became intolerable for me I began to go about in society so that I too would not fall prey to madness. For the sake of the child I had to preserve some state of normalcy in the household.

I was not prepared for the rush of sentiments which overcame me upon meeting you. I was overjoyed to think that perhaps life still had some meaning for me. While I knew that eventually I would have to confess all this, in weakness I put it off.

You broke my heart when you rushed away upon learning that I was married. I do not know what tragedy would have befallen me if you had refused to speak to me the next day.

We tried to be rational. When we discussed the possibility of your coming to Morelands as governess to my daughter, you said I was asking the impossible. You said you could not face your family if you came to live in my home. But can you not present it to them as just a simple work situation? If you did not tell them who I was, it would merely be an omission and not a fabrication.

My darling, won't you reconsider? Go back to America as you planned. Think it over carefully. Then return to me here at Morelands, confident in the knowledge that I will never love another as I love you. I know in my heart that you share these feelings. I beg you to consider that we could at least have the pleasure of each other's company while we await the day you can become my wife. I assure you I would not act with any impropriety. And of course Edwina would benefit from your gentle teaching. Please, my darling, come to Morelands. I cannot bear to lose you.

Whatever transpires, I am sending these jewels as my gift to you. They are only a symbol of my deepest feelings. Do whatever you want with them, but do not send them back as I will immediately return them to you. They are yours.

My undying love,
Edwin"

When Sarah had finished reading the letter, she was silent. There was a funny lump in her throat. Even the boys were not able to speak. "She couldn't resist him," said Martha with a small sniffle.

"Cousin Felicity was right," Sam said. "Philippa kept Morelands a secret from her family. That's why she kept 'losing' things like the doll. She was bringing them to England to Edwin and Edwina Moreland."

Sarah solemnly took off the diamond tiara and wrapped it up with the other jewels in her sweater. She handed Sam the iron box to carry.

"It's all so sad. I'm glad we have that letter. I knew Philippa wasn't sending me on a wild goose chase. There was something to all those messages and signs, after all." As they started walking back to the house, Sarah turned to Sam. "I'm so happy to know for sure that Philippa never stole the jewels. I hate to say I told you so, but now do you believe me?"

❧21❧

Philippa at Rest

Mrs. Bingham had put away her writing and was in the kitchen arranging some flowers. She was carefully guiding an aster into the vase when the four young people entered the kitchen. Glancing curiously at Sarah, she wondered why she was so tightly clutching her rolled-up sweater.

Setting the sweater gently on the table, Sarah said, "Mom, we found it! But you better sit down before we show it to you!"

"Found what?" asked Mrs. Bingham, as she calmly snipped the stem of a zinnia.

"Philippa's jewels. The 'something valuable' she mentioned in the letter to Evangeline. The treasure she was urging me to seek."

"But Evangeline never found it!" said Sam. "Sarah and John figured out the code when they went to the library and we followed the clues until we found it! We have the Moreland family jewels! Right here, inside that sweater!"

Mrs. Bingham was looking more baffled than ever. "Whatever are you talking about? I don't understand a word you're saying!"

"That's why I was always thinking about Philippa, Mom," said Sarah. "I knew there had to be a reason I discovered the letters when I did. And then Mrs. Chaney appeared with the locket. And then I had those dreams about Philippa. And then I found the doll in the antique store, and finally we solved the code! It was all leading up to this. It's very clear to me now."

Sam saw that the rush of words spilling out of Sarah was confusing their mother even more. "Sarah is trying to tell you that she really believes that the spirit of Philippa was leading her on to look for something she had hidden."

By now Sarah had unrolled her sweater and opened the packet of jewels. There they lay, an unbelievable treasure, shining gloriously on the rough wool of her sweater.

Mrs. Bingham dropped the zinnia, her cutting shears, and her jaw. Astonishment flooded her face. She was totally unprepared for such a sight! She stared in amazement at the pile of magnificent jewelry. "What

. . . where . . . where did they come from?" she finally asked.

Sarah handed her mother the letter. They all stood around admiring the jewelry while Mrs. Bingham read it. No one noticed that Mr. and Mrs. Chaney had entered the room.

"We wondered where everybody—oh, my goodness gracious, what have we here?" asked the incredulous Mrs. Chaney when she spotted the jewelry on the table.

"Then," said Mrs. Bingham, "these jewels would actually belong to the Bingham family, according to this letter. Philippa's heirs could legitimately claim them since we have it in Edwin Moreland's handwriting that he gave them to Philippa."

"Philippa probably left the letter there for her sister to read for just that reason," said Samuel. "She must have had a hard time thinking of a way to let Evangeline know how she had come by all this jewelry. I bet she finally decided it would be easier to just let Edwin's letter speak for itself. After all, Philippa hadn't ever told Evangeline she was living at Morelands. She let her believe it was any old job."

"Of course she couldn't tell Evangeline the truth in those days," said Sarah. "Evangeline would not have approved of her sister's living in the same house with Edwin Moreland."

"But Philippa couldn't just stand by and let Evangeline suffer when she had this fortune hidden away on the property," Sam speculated.

"The innkeeper said Philippa met with a suspicious accident." said Sarah. "Do you suppose Edwin's wife or one of the servants tampered with Philippa's horse so it would fall when she was riding it?"

"Maybe there was some jealousy at work," said Martha, looking at the portrait of Edwin Moreland in the locket. "He was very handsome."

"Or disapproval," said Sam. "Maybe someone in the household didn't like Philippa's being there. After all, Edwin Moreland still had a wife, no matter what condition she was in."

"Maybe she just stumbled and had a natural fall," said John. "Even the best riders have accidents."

"We'll never know what happened," said Mrs. Bingham as she watched Mrs. Chaney pick up the locket with the portrait of Edwin Moreland in it.

"This is incredible," said Mrs. Chaney. "Except for the portrait, this locket is an exact duplicate of mine."

"It was quite common for people to exchange portraits with their loved ones back in the 1800s," said Mr. Chaney.

"These jewels are so valuable that we'll have to sell them. I can't believe it! Now we'll have enough money to fix the roof and renovate the barn and still have plenty left over to save for your college educations!" said Mrs. Bingham.

"Not the locket, Mom," begged Sarah. "Please don't sell the locket. Can't I keep just this one piece? It would mean so much to me."

Mrs. Bingham smiled. "Of course you can keep the locket, Sarah. I think it would be very fitting for you to have it. And it's something you can wear. Even if we didn't need the money these jewels will bring us, we couldn't keep them. They're much too fancy for us. They belong in a museum."

Mrs. Chaney had taken off her own locket from around her neck. After carefully comparing the two portraits, she turned to Sarah. "Which of these two lockets would you rather own, my dear?" she asked.

"Why, the one with Philippa's portrait in it, of course," answered Sarah immediately. "But that one is yours!"

"Well, Sarah," Mrs. Chaney said gently, "I don't really care which portrait I have in my locket. They're both beautiful work. And the lockets are identical. You can exchange yours for mine if you'd like," she offered.

"Oh, Mrs. Chaney, that's so nice of you," said Sarah as Mrs. Chaney draped the locket with the portrait of Philippa around her neck. Pushing open the spring, she made the portrait pop into view. Philippa's face, so like her own, was looking back at her. Admiring it happily, Sarah said, "I'll wear it all the time. And Philippa will always be with me."

Mrs. Bingham put her arm around Sarah. "I guess you were right to delve into Philippa's letters so carefully. They led you to quite a spectacular find. Can you forgive me for trying to make you stop thinking about her?"

"Oh, Mom, don't be silly. I know you were only thinking of my own good!" said Sarah.

"True," said her mother as she began carefully wrapping up the precious jewels. "And now the jewels will be for the whole family's good! Why, this is some windfall! It's like winning the lottery!"

The others were all excitedly talking about the wonderful jewelry. No one was paying any attention to Sarah, who was still staring at the portrait of Philippa.

Had she imagined it? Was she dreaming again? Or was that a gentle smile she saw flitting across Philippa's face? "That's enough now, Philippa," she whispered. "We've cleared your name. Your jewels will help us. Now, rest in peace."

Firmly she snapped the locket shut.

ABOUT THE AUTHOR

ANNE GRAHAM ESTERN has been an art teacher, a doll designer, a scenic designer, an art director, and a producer of children's television shows. Her first two books for young readers, *The Picolinis* and *The Picolinis and the Haunted House*, were also published by Bantam Books.

In *Letters from Philippa*, her third book, Ms. Estern has combined her interest in fantasy and the supernatural with her love for the New England countryside, Early American art, antiques, and sturdy Yankee courage.

Anne Estern and her husband, Neil, a sculptor, have three grown children. They divide their time between an old farmhouse in Connecticut and an even older brownstone house in Brooklyn, New York.

Are you a good detective?
Solve tricky mysteries with
ENCYCLOPEDIA BROWN!
by Donald Sobol

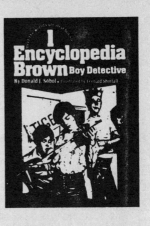

Match wits with the great sleuth in sneakers Leroy (Encyclopedia) Brown! Each Encyclopedia Brown book contains ten baffling cases for you to solve. You'll find mysteries such as "The Case of the Worm Pills" and "The Case of the Masked Robber."

Get ready for fun with the great detective! You'll want to solve each one of these mysteries. Order today!